Georges Simenon

Maigret and the Killer

Georges Simenon

Maigret and the Killer

Translated from the French by Lyn Moir

A HARVEST/HBJ BOOK
A Helen and Kurt Wolff Book
Harcourt Brace Jovanovich
NEW YORK AND LONDON

Copyright © 1969 by Georges Simenon
English translation copyright © 1971 by Georges Simenon

All rights reserved. No part of
this publication may be reproduced or
transmitted in any form or by any means,
electronic or mechanical, including photocopy,
recording, or any information storage and
retrieval system, without permission
in writing from the publisher.

Printed in the United States of America

LIBRARY OF CONGRESS CATALOGING IN PUBLICATION DATA
Simenon, Georges, 1903–
Maigret and the killer.
(A Harvest/HBJ book)
"A Helen and Kurt Wolff book."
Translation of Maigret et le tueur.
I. Title.
PZ3.S5892Maego   1979   [PQ2637.I53]   843'.9'12   79-10402
ISBN 0-15-655124-1

First Harvest/HBJ edition 1979

A B C D E F G H I J

Georges Simenon

Maigret and the Killer

Chapter **1**   For the first time since they had
started dining once a month at the Pardons, Maigret
would keep an unpleasant memory of the evening on the
Boulevard Voltaire.

It had begun on the Boulevard Richard-Lenoir. His
wife had phoned for a taxi because it had been raining for
three days, harder, according to the radio, than it had
rained for thirty-five years. The rain was pouring down,
icy cold, slapping one's face and hands, plastering the wet
clothes to one's body.

On stairs, in elevators and offices, feet left muddy marks
and people were in a vile mood.

They had gone downstairs and had waited almost half
an hour at the door of the building, getting more and
more chilled, for the taxi to arrive. Even then he had had
to argue to get the driver to take such a short trip.

"Do forgive us. We're late."

"Everyone's late on days like this. I hope you won't
mind sitting down to dinner right away."

The apartment was warm, friendly, and it felt even co-
zier with the wind making the shutters bang. Madame Pardon had made a *boeuf bourguignon* as only she could, and
this dish, delicate and satisfying at the same time, had
taken up much of the conversation.

Then they had talked about provincial cooking, cassou-
let, *potée lorraine, tripes à la mode de Caen,* bouilla-
baisse. . . .

"After all, most of these recipes grew out of necessity

3

—if there had been refrigerators right from the Middle Ages . . ."

What else had they talked about? The two women, as usual, had ended up by installing themselves in a corner of the room, where they talked in low tones. Pardon had taken Maigret into his office to show him a rare book that had been given to him by one of his patients. They had sat down without thinking and Madame Pardon had taken their coffee and calvados in to them.

Pardon was tired. For quite some time his features had been drawn and sometimes there was an expression of something like resignation in his eyes. He still worked a fifteen-hour day, at least, never complaining or finding fault, spending the mornings in his office, part of the afternoons dragging his heavy bag from street to street, then back home again to a waiting room that was always full.

"If I had a son and he told me he wanted to be a doctor, I think I'd try to dissuade him."

Maigret almost turned his face away out of sheer embarrassment. It was the most unexpected thing to hear from Pardon's lips, for he was in love with his profession and one couldn't imagine him doing anything else.

This time he was discouraged, pessimistic, and, what was more, he went so far as to put his pessimism into words.

"They're trying to turn us into clerks and change medicine into a vast computer giving out more or less adequate cures."

Maigret, lighting his pipe, watched him.

"Not only into clerks," went on the doctor, "but bad clerks, for we can't give the necessary time to every patient. Sometimes I'm ashamed as I see them to the door, almost shoving them out. I see the look in their eyes— worried, imploring even. I know that they expect something else of me, questions, words, in fact time that I can devote to their case alone. . . ."

He lifted his glass.

"Your health."

He forced a smile, a mechanical smile that did not suit him.

"Do you know how many patients I've seen today? Eighty-two. And that's not unusual. After which I am obliged to fill out various forms. That takes up my evenings. I'm sorry to bore you with this. You must have your own problems at the Quai des Orfèvres."

What had they talked about after that? Nothing memorable. Pardon sat at his desk, smoking a cigarette, Maigret in the straight chair used by the patients. A particular smell pervaded the room, one which the superintendent knew well, for he smelled it on each of his visits. A smell that somehow brought to mind that of a police station. The smell of poverty.

Pardon's patients were local people, almost all of low income.

The door opened. Eugénie, the maid, who had worked so long in the household on the Boulevard Voltaire that she was almost part of the family, announced:

"It's the Italian, Doctor."

"Which Italian? Pagliati?"

"Yes, Doctor. He's in a terrible state. He says it's very urgent."

It was half past ten. Pardon got up, opened the door into the dismal waiting room with magazines scattered over a table.

"What's wrong, Gino?"

"It's not me, Doctor. Nor my wife. There's a man lying wounded on the sidewalk, who must be dying."

"Where?"

"On the Rue Popincourt, a hundred yards away."

"Were you the first to find him?"

Pardon was already in the hall, putting on his black overcoat, looking for his bag, and Maigret instinctively put his coat on too. The doctor opened the dining-room door.

"We'll be right back. There's a wounded man on the Rue Popincourt."

"Take your umbrella."

He didn't take it. He would have felt ridiculous holding an umbrella and leaning over a man dying in the middle of the sidewalk with the rain pattering all around.

Gino was a Neapolitan. He had a small grocery store at the corner of the Rue du Chemin-Vert and the Rue Popincourt. Or, more exactly, it was his wife, Lucia, who kept the shop while he made fresh noodles, ravioli, tortellini. The couple were well liked in the district. Pardon had treated Gino for high blood pressure.

The noodle-maker was a short man, stockily built, heavy, with a ruddy complexion.

"We were coming back from my brother-in-law's on the Rue de Charonne. My sister-in-law's going to have a baby and he's expecting to take her to the lying-in hospital at any moment. . . . We were walking home in the rain when I saw . . ."

Half of his words were lost in the storm. The gutters had become rushing streams that had to be jumped over, and the few passing cars threw up sprays of dirty water for several yards.

The sight that greeted them on the Rue Popincourt was unexpected. There wasn't anyone walking, from one end of the street to the other, and only a few windows, apart from those of a little café, were still lit.

About fifty yards from the café a stoutish woman was

standing motionless under an umbrella shaken by the wind. A street lamp showed up the shape of a body lying at her feet.

That brought back old memories to Maigret. Long before he was head of the Criminal Division, while he was only a detective, he often happened to be the first at the scene of a brawl, of a settling of accounts, of an armed attack.

The man was young. He looked hardly twenty; he wore a suède jacket and had fairly long hair. He had fallen on his face and the back of his jacket was caked with blood.

"Have you notified the police?"

Pardon, bent close over the wounded man, interrupted:

"Get them to send an ambulance."

That meant that the unknown man was alive, and Maigret went toward the light that he saw fifty yards away. On the faintly lit shop front were the words "Chez Jules." He pushed open the glass door, which had a cream-colored curtain stretched over it, and went in to an atmosphere so calm that it seemed unreal. It might have been a genre painting.

It was an old-fashioned bar, with sawdust on the floor and a strong smell of wine and liquor. Four oldish men, three of them fat and red-faced, were playing cards.

"May I use the telephone?"

In amazement they watched him go over to the wall telephone which was near the zinc counter and the rows of bottles.

"Hello. Is that the 11th arrondissement police station?"

It was a stone's throw away, on the Place Léon-Blum, which used to be called the Place Voltaire.

"Hello. This is Maigret. There's a man lying wounded on the Rue Popincourt. Near the Rue du Chemin-Vert. Send an ambulance."

The four men came to life as if they were actors on a stage. They kept their cards in their hands.

"What's that?" asked the one in shirt sleeves, who must have been the proprietor. "Who's wounded?"

"A young man."

Maigret put the money on the counter and went toward the door.

"A tall, thin fellow in a suède jacket?"

"Yes."

"He was in here a quarter of an hour ago."

"Alone?"

"Yes."

"Did he seem nervous?"

The proprietor, obviously Jules, gave the others a questioning look.

"No, not especially."

"Did he stay long?"

"About twenty minutes."

When Maigret went out again he saw two policemen with bicycles, the rain pouring down their capes, standing beside the wounded man. Pardon had stood up again.

"There's nothing I can do. He's been stabbed several times. The heart has not been touched. No artery has been cut either, as far as I can see, or there would have been more blood."

"Will he regain consciousness?"

"I don't know. I don't dare move him. We can only see once we get him to the hospital."

The two vehicles, the police car and the ambulance, arrived at almost the same time. The card players, rather than get wet, stood in the doorway of the little café and watched from a distance. Only the proprietor came forward, wearing a sack over his head and shoulders. He recognized the jacket immediately.

"It's definitely him."

"Did he say anything to you?"

"No. Only ordered a brandy. . . ."

Pardon was giving instructions to the ambulance men carrying their stretcher.

"What's that?" asked one of the policemen, pointing to a black object that looked rather like a camera.

The wounded man was carrying it on a strap around his neck. It was not a camera but a cassette tape recorder. The rain was soaking it, and when they slid the man onto the stretcher, Maigret took advantage of the situation to undo the strap.

"To Saint-Antoine Hospital."

Pardon got into the back of the ambulance with one of the men while the other drove.

"What are you?" the driver asked Maigret.

"Police."

"Come up here with me."

The streets were deserted, and less than five minutes later the ambulance, followed by one of the police cars, arrived at Saint-Antoine Hospital.

Here too Maigret found old memories surging back— the light shining over the door open day and night, the long, badly lit corridor where two or three uncomplaining people waited silently on the benches, jumping up each time a door opened and closed again, each time a man or woman in white went from one place to another.

"Do you have his name and address?" asked a sister enclosed in a glass cage with a small opening.

"Not yet."

An intern, alerted by a bell, came from the end of the corridor, regretfully stubbing out a cigarette. Pardon introduced himself.

"You've done nothing?"

The wounded man, laid out on a stretcher, was pushed into an elevator, and Pardon, following him, signaled vaguely to Maigret from a distance, as if saying:

"I'll be right back."

"Do you know anything, Superintendent?"

"No more than you do. I was dining at a friend's house nearby when someone came to tell my friend, who's a doctor, that there was a wounded man lying on the sidewalk on the Rue Popincourt."

The policeman noted this down in his book. Less than ten minutes had passed in a disagreeable silence when Pardon appeared at the end of the corridor. It was a bad sign. The doctor's face was worried.

"Dead?"

"Before he could even be undressed. Hemorrhage in the lung cavity. I was afraid of that when I heard his breathing."

"Stab wounds?"

"Yes. Several. A fairly thin blade. In a few minutes they'll bring you the contents of his pockets. Then I suppose he'll be sent to the Forensic Institute?"

This Paris was familiar to Maigret. He had lived in it for years and yet he had never grown completely accustomed to it. What was he doing here? A stab wound, several stab wounds—they were none of his business. Such things happened every night and in the morning they were written off in three or four lines in the daily reports.

Chance had had it that this evening he was in the stalls, and suddenly he felt himself a little part of it. The Italian noodle-maker had not had the time to tell him what he had seen. He must have gone home with his wife. They slept on the first floor, above the shop.

A nurse was walking toward the little group, a basket in her hand.

"Who is in charge of the case?"

The plain-clothes men looked at Maigret, and it was to him that she spoke:

"Here is what was found in his pockets. You'll have to sign a receipt."

There was a small wallet, one of those that slip into the hip pocket, a ball-point pen, a pipe, a tobacco pouch with very pale Dutch tobacco in it, a handkerchief, some change, and two cassette tapes.

In the wallet an identity card and driver's license in the name of Antoine Batille, twenty-one years old, address Quai d'Anjou, Paris. That was on the Ile Saint-Louis, not far from the Pont-Marie. There was also a student's card.

"Pardon, would you ask my wife to go home without me and go to bed?"

"Are you going there?"

"I have to. He obviously lives with his parents, and I must tell them."

He turned to the policemen.

"See what information you can get from Pagliati, the Italian grocer on the Rue Popincourt, and the four men who were playing cards in Chez Jules, if they're still at the café."

As always, he was sorry not to be able to do everything himself. He would have liked to go back to the Rue Popincourt, push open the door of the café where the smoke gathered around the electric light and where the card players had probably gone on with their game.

He would have liked, too, to question the Italian and his wife, and possibly a little old woman whom he had only glimpsed at the lighted window on the first floor of one of the houses. Had she been there when the drama took place?

But first he had to notify the parents. He telephoned

11

the duty sergeant of the 11th arrondissement and informed him of the situation.

"Did he suffer very much?" he asked Pardon.

"I don't think so. He lost consciousness immediately. I couldn't do anything there on the sidewalk."

The wallet was of excellent quality crocodile, the ballpoint pen was silver, the handkerchief bore the hand-embroidered initial "A."

"Would you be so kind as to call me a taxi, Madame?"

She did it, from her cage, without any kindness. It was true that it couldn't be very pleasant to spend all one's nights in such a dismal place waiting for the tragedies of the district to come to an end at the hospital.

By a miracle, the taxi arrived less than three minutes later.

"I'll see you home, Pardon."

"Don't wait for me."

"Well, you know, with news like mine . . ."

He knew the Ile Saint-Louis fairly well since he used to live on the Place des Vosges, and at that time they often walked arm in arm around the island in the evening.

He rang at a green-painted door. Cars were parked all along the sides of the street, most of them very expensive. A narrow door within the big one opened.

"Monsieur Batille, please?" he asked, stopping at a small window in the wall.

The sleepy voice of a woman answered simply:

"Second floor on the left."

He took the elevator, and some of the rain that had soaked right through his overcoat and trousers made a puddle at his feet. The building, like most of those on the island, had been restored. The walls were of white stone, the lighting by bronze candelabra. On the marble landing, the doormat had a large red letter "B."

He rang and heard an electric bell far in the distance, but it was a long time before the door opened silently.

A young maid in a smart uniform looked at him curiously.

"I would like to speak to Monsieur Batille."

"Father or son?"

"The father."

"Monsieur and Madame are not back yet and I don't know at what time they will return."

He showed his police identity badge.

"What is it about?" she asked.

"I am Superintendent Maigret, of the Criminal Police."

"And you have come to see Monsieur at this time of night? Is he expecting you?"

"No."

"Is it very urgent?"

"It is important."

"It's almost midnight. Monsieur and Madame went to the theater."

"In that case, they are likely to be returning soon."

"Unless they go to have supper with friends afterward, as they often do."

"Did young Monsieur Batille not go with them?"

"He never goes anywhere with them."

He could feel that she was embarrassed. She did not know what to make of him, and he must be a terrible sight, dripping with water. He glimpsed a huge hall, the floor covered completely with a pale blue carpet with a hint of green in it.

"If it's really urgent . . ."

She resigned herself to letting him in.

"Let me have your hat and coat."

She gave his shoes a worried look. She could not, however, ask him to take them off.

"This way."

She hung the coat in a cloakroom and hesitated before showing Maigret into the large drawing room that opened on the left.

"You won't mind waiting in here?"

He understood very well what she meant. The luxurious appearance of the apartment was almost too refined, rather feminine. The armchairs in the drawing room were white and the pictures on the walls were Picassos of the blue period, Renoirs, and Marie Laurencins.

The maid, who was young and pretty, was visibly wondering if she ought to leave him alone or keep an eye on him, as if she were not too sure of the badge he had shown her.

"Is Monsieur Batille in business?"

"Don't you know him?"

"No."

"You don't know that he is the owner of Mylène perfumes and beauty aids?"

He knew so little about aids to beauty! And Madame Maigret, who only used a little powder, was not the woman to keep him informed about such things.

"How old is he?"

"Forty-five? Forty-six? He looks very young."

She blushed. She must be more or less in love with her employer.

"And his wife?"

"If you lean forward a little you will see her portrait, over the mantelpiece."

In a blue evening dress. Pale blue and pink seemed to be the colors of the house, as in the Marie Laurencin paintings.

"I think I can hear the elevator."

And, in spite of herself, she breathed a slight sigh of relief.

She spoke to them in a low voice, near the door toward which she had hurried. They were a young couple, elegant, with no apparent cares, returning home after an evening at the theater. First one and then the other looked from a distance at the intruder with soaking trousers and shoes who had risen awkwardly from his chair and who was wondering what expression to put on.

The man took off his gray coat under which he was wearing a dinner jacket. His wife, under her leopard-skin coat, had on a cocktail dress made of silver lamé.

They had about ten yards to walk, perhaps less. Batille walked in front, his steps quick and nervous. His wife followed him.

"I'm told you are Superintendent Maigret," he murmured, frowning.

"That is correct."

"If I am not mistaken, you are the head of the Criminal Division."

There was a short, rather unpleasant silence during which Madame Batille was trying to guess what had happened. She was no longer in the same gay mood in which she had entered a few moments earlier.

"It's odd that you should come at this time of night. Would it be about my son, by any chance?"

"Were you expecting to hear bad news about him?"

"Not at all. Let's not stay here. Let's go into my study."

It was the end room, opening off the drawing room. Batille's office must be somewhere else, in the Mylène Products building, which Maigret had often noticed on the Avenue Matignon.

The bookcases were of pale wood, lemon-wood or maple, and the walls were lined with books. The leather armchairs were a soft beige, as were the accessories on the desk. On the desk were photographs in a silver frame—Madame Batille, and the heads of two children, a boy and a girl.

"Sit down. Have you been waiting long?"

"Only ten minutes or so."

"Will you have something to drink?"

"No, thank you."

It seemed now as if the man was putting off hearing what the superintendent had to say to him.

"Have you had no problems with your son?"

He appeared to reflect for a moment.

"No. He's a quiet boy, and reserved. Perhaps too quiet and reserved."

"What do you think of his friends?"

"He has hardly any friends. He's quite the opposite of his sister, who is only eighteen and makes friends easily. He has no close friends, no friends at all. Has anything happened to him?"

"Yes."

"Has he had an accident?"

"You might call it that. He was attacked this evening, in the dark, on the Rue Popincourt."

"Was he wounded?"

"Yes."

"Badly?"

"He is dead."

Maigret would have preferred not to see them, not to be present at this sudden disintegration. The society couple, full of self-assurance and ease, disappeared. Their clothes no longer looked as if they came from a couturier or a high-class tailor. The apartment itself lost its elegance and charm.

All that remained was a man and a woman, shattered with grief, who were still battling not to believe the news they had just been given.

"Are you sure it is my . . ."

"He is Antoine Batille, isn't he?"

Maigret held out the still sodden wallet.

"Yes, that is his."

Batille lit a cigarette mechanically. His hands were trembling. His lips too.

"How did it happen?"

"He had just left a small local bar. He had gone about fifty yards in the pouring rain and someone stabbed him several times, from behind."

The woman grimaced as if she had been the one to be stabbed and her husband put his arm around her shoulders. He tried to speak but could not, at first. What was there to say, anyway? The things that were passing through his head, even if they were not what he was really worried about?

"Have they caught the . . ."

"No."

"Did he die immediately?"

"As soon as he got to Saint-Antoine Hospital."

"May we go to see him?"

"I would advise you not to go there tonight but to wait until the morning."

"Did he suffer?"

"The doctor says not."

"Go to bed, Martine. Lie down on your bed, at least."

He led her away gently but firmly.

"I shall be with you in a moment, Superintendent."

Batille was gone for almost a quarter of an hour, and when he returned he was very pale, his face drawn and his eyes expressionless.

"Do sit down."

He was a small man, thin and nervous. One got the impression that Maigret's vast, heavy bulk upset him.

"Are you sure you won't have anything to drink?"

He opened a little cocktail cabinet and took out a bottle and two glasses.

"I must admit I need one."

He poured himself a whisky and poured some into the second glass.

"Much soda?"

And, immediately:

"I don't understand. I just can't understand it. Antoine was a boy who didn't keep anything from me, and, besides, there was nothing in his life to hide. He was . . . It's hard for me to speak of him in the past tense, but I must get used to it. He was a student. He was studying for an Arts degree at the Sorbonne. He didn't belong to any particular group. He wasn't interested, not even slightly, in politics."

He gazed at the snuff-colored carpet, his arms hanging loosely, and spoke to himself:

"Somebody killed my boy. . . . Why? . . . But why?"

"That's what I'm here to try to find out."

Batille looked at Maigret as if seeing him for the first time.

"Why have you come yourself? As far as the police are concerned, it's just an everyday occurrence, isn't it?"

"As luck would have it, I was almost on the spot."

"Did you see anything?"

"No."

"Didn't anybody see anything?"

"An Italian grocer, who was on his way home with his wife. I have brought you the things that were found in your son's pockets, but I forgot his tape recorder."

The father seemed not to understand right away, then he murmured:

"Oh, yes. . . ."

He gave a half-smile.

"It was his passion. You'll probably laugh. His sister and I teased him too. Some people are mad about photography and go hunting for striking faces, even under the bridges. Antoine collected human voices. He often spent whole evenings at it. He would go into cafés, into stations, any public place, and turn on his tape recorder. He wore it on his chest, and many people thought it was a camera. He concealed a miniature microphone with his hand."

Maigret had something to get hold of at last.

"Did he ever have any trouble?"

"Only once. It was in a bar somewhere near Les Ternes. Two men were leaning at the counter. Antoine was standing beside them and recording surreptitiously.

" 'Here, boy,' one of them said suddenly. He took the tape recorder away from him and removed the cassette.

" 'I don't know what you're playing at, but if I see you around here again, make sure you don't have that thing with you.' "

Gérard Batille took a drink and spoke again.

"Do you think that . . ."

"Anything is possible. We can't risk making any assumptions. Did he often go out hunting voices?"

"Two or three times a week."

"Always by himself?"

"I've already told you he didn't have any friends. He called these recordings human documents."

"Are there a lot of them?"

"Maybe a hundred, maybe more. He listened to them from time to time and erased the ones that weren't so good. What time tomorrow, do you think?"

"I'll tell the hospital you are coming. Not before eight o'clock, in any case."

"Shall I be able to bring the body home?"

"Not right away."

The father understood, and his face grew even grayer as he imagined the autopsy.

"Forgive me, Superintendent, but I . . ."

He could take no more. He needed to be alone, or perhaps to rejoin his wife, perhaps to weep or to cry out in the silence of words that find no echo.

He said, as if to himself: "I don't know when Minou will come in."

"Who is that?"

"His sister. She's only eighteen, but she lives her own life. I suppose you had a coat?"

The maid appeared just as they reached the cloakroom and helped Maigret into his sodden coat and handed him his hat.

He went downstairs, then opened the little door and waited a full minute in the doorway, watching the rain fall. The wind seemed to have dropped a little, the squalls of rain to be less fierce. He had not ventured to ask permission to telephone for a taxi.

Shoulders hunched, he crossed the Pont-Marie, went down the narrow Rue Saint-Paul, and finally found a taxi in a rank near the Saint-Paul métro station.

"Boulevard Richard-Lenoir."

"Right, Chief."

A driver who knew him and who didn't complain that the distance was too short. Raising his head when he got out of the car, he saw the lighted windows of his apartment. As he climbed the last flight of stairs, the door opened.

"You haven't caught a cold?"

"I don't think so."

"I have the water boiling to make you a toddy. Sit down. Let me take your shoes off."

His socks were wringing wet. She went to find his slippers.

"Pardon told his wife and me what had happened. How did his parents react? Why was it you who . . ."

"I don't know."

He had become involved in this case involuntarily, because he had almost fallen over it, because it reminded him of many years spent in the streets of Paris at night.

"They didn't take it in right away. It's only now that they must both be feeling the strain."

"Are they young?"

"The man must be a bit more than forty-five, but I think he's less than fifty. As for his wife, she hardly looks forty and she's very pretty. You know Mylène perfumes?"

"Of course. Everyone does."

"Well, then, that's who they are."

"They're very rich. They have a château in Sologne, a yacht at Cannes, and they give fabulous parties."

"How do you know?"

"Are you forgetting that I have to spend a lot of time waiting for you and I sometimes read the gossip columns in the papers?"

She poured some rum into a glass, put in some sugar, left the spoon in so that the glass wouldn't crack, and poured in some boiling water.

"A slice of lemon?"

"No."

The room around him was small, narrow. He looked at

the décor like someone who has just returned from a long trip.

"What are you thinking about?"

"As you said, they're very rich. They have one of the most luxurious apartments I've ever seen. They were coming back from the theater, still in high spirits. . . . They saw me sitting at the end of the hall. . . . The maid whispered to them who I was. . . ."

"Get undressed."

After all, wasn't it better here? He put on his pajamas, brushed his teeth, and a quarter of an hour later, his head a bit light after the toddy, he was lying in bed beside Madame Maigret.

"Good night," she said, putting her face close to his.

He kissed her as he had done for many years and murmured "Good night."

"As usual?"

That meant "Shall I wake you at half past seven as usual with a cup of coffee?"

His grunted "yes" was already blurred, for sleep came upon him suddenly. He did not dream. Or, if he did, he didn't remember it. And all at once it was morning.

While he sat in bed drinking his coffee and his wife parted the curtains, he tried to see through the net half-curtains.

"Is it still raining?"

"No. But from the way people are walking with their hands in their pockets, it isn't spring yet, whatever the calendar may say."

It was the 19th of March. A Wednesday. His first task, when he had put on his dressing gown, was to ring Saint-Antoine Hospital, and he had the greatest difficulty getting put through to anyone in administration.

"Yes. . . . I want him to be put in a private room. . . .

I know perfectly well he is dead. . . . That's no reason why the parents should have to see him in the basement. . . . They'll be there in an hour or two. . . . After they have gone, his body will be taken to the Forensic Institute. Yes. Don't worry. . . . The family will pay. . . . Yes, of course. . . . They will fill out all the forms you like. . . ."

He sat down opposite his wife and had two croissants as he drank another cup of coffee and stared mechanically at the street. Low-lying clouds still scudded across the sky, but they were not the same unhealthy color as on the previous day. The wind, still strong, shook the branches of the trees.

"Do you have any idea . . ."

"You know very well I never have any ideas."

"And if you do, you don't talk about them. Didn't you think Pardon looked ill?"

"Did that strike you too? He's not just tired, he has become a pessimist. Yesterday he spoke to me about his profession in a way he has never done before."

At nine o'clock he was in his office calling the 11th arrondissement police station.

"Maigret here. Is that you, Louvelle?"

He had recognized his voice.

"I expect you're calling about the tape recorder."

"Yes. Do you have it?"

"Demarie picked it up and brought it here. I was afraid that the rain might have ruined it, but I got it to work. I wonder why the boy recorded those conversations."

"Can you send me the tape recorder this morning?"

"When I send the report, which will be typed in a few minutes."

The mail. Paperwork. He had not told Pardon the previous evening that he too was snowed under with administrative paperwork.

Then he went to the briefing, in the director's office. He gave a summary of what had happened the night before, since the case was likely to get a lot of publicity because of who Gérard Batille was.

In fact, when he returned to his office he ran into a crowd of newspapermen and photographers.

"Is it true that you almost witnessed the murder?"

"I arrived on the scene so quickly only because I was nearby at the time."

"This boy, Antoine Batille, is he really the son of Batille the perfume manufacturer?"

How had the press found out? Had the leak come from the police station?

"The concierge says . . ."

"What concierge?"

"The one at the house on the Quai d'Anjou."

He hadn't even seen her. He hadn't given his name or his rank. The maid must have told her.

"It was you who broke the news to the parents, wasn't it?"

"Yes."

"What was their reaction?"

"The same as that of any man and woman who are told that their son has been killed."

"Have they any idea who did it?"

"No."

"You don't think it could be a political killing?"

"Certainly not."

"Something to do with a love affair, then?"

"I don't think so."

"He wasn't robbed, was he?"

"No."

"Well, then?"

"Well nothing, gentlemen. The investigation is only beginning, and when it brings in some results I'll give you the information."

"Have you seen the daughter?"

"Who?"

"Minou. The Batilles' daughter. She seems to be well known in certain interesting circles."

"No, I haven't seen her."

"She has some very strange friends."

"Thank you for telling me, but I'm not investigating her."

"One never knows, does one?"

He brushed them aside, opened the door of his office, and shut it behind him. He stood in front of the window while he filled his pipe, then he went into the inspectors' office. They were not all there. Some of them were telephoning, others working at their typewriters.

"Are you busy, Janvier?"

"Ten more lines to type, Chief, and I'll have finished my report."

"Come and see me then."

While he waited, he called up the forensic surgeon who had succeeded his old friend Doctor Paul.

"He'll be sent over to you later in the morning. It's an urgent case, not because of what I expect to hear from the autopsy, but because of the parents' impatience. . . . Mess him up as little as possible. . . . Yes. . . . That's right. . . . I can see you understand. Most of Parisian society will be paying its respects to the body. . . . There are already newspapermen outside in the corridor here."

The first thing he had to do was to go to the Rue Popincourt. Gino Pagliati hadn't had time to say much the previous evening and his wife had scarcely opened her mouth at all. Then there was the man called Jules and the three other card players. Finally, Maigret had not forgotten the silhouette of the old woman he had seen at the window.

"What are we doing, Chief?" asked Janvier as he came into the office.

"Is there a free car in the car park?"

"I hope so."

"Drive me to the Rue Popincourt. Not far from the Rue du Chemin-Vert. I'll tell you when to stop."

His wife was right, he realized while he waited in the middle of the courtyard for the car: it was cold enough for December.

Chapter 2   Maigret realized that even Janvier was
a little surprised at the importance given to this case.
Every night there are a certain number of stabbings recorded in one or another part of Paris, particularly in the
poorer districts, and ordinarily the papers would have
given only a few lines to the tragedy on the Rue Popincourt, under the heading of "News in Brief."

STABBING

"A young man, Antoine B . . . , 21 years old,
student, was stabbed several times as he walked
along the Rue Popincourt at about 10:30 on
Tuesday evening. It appears that it was an attempted robbery but the arrival of a man and
wife, local shopkeepers, on the scene stopped
the man from stripping his victim. Antoine B . . .
died on arrival at Saint-Antoine Hospital."

But Antoine B . . . was called Antoine Batille and
lived on the Quai d'Anjou. His father was a well-known
man, a prominent figure in society, and everyone had heard
of the Mylène perfumes.

The little black car from the Criminal Police crossed
the Place de la République and Maigret found himself in
his own district, a network of narrow streets, heavily pop-
ulated, bounded by the Boulevard Voltaire on one side
and the Boulevard Richard-Lenoir on the other.

Madame Maigret and he walked along these little
streets each time they went to the Pardons' for dinner,
and Madame Maigret often did her shopping on the Rue
du Chemin-Vert.

27

It was at Gino's, as it was called familiarly, that she bought not only pasta but mortadella, prosciutto, and olive oil in large, golden-colored cans. The shops were narrow, deep, and badly lit. Today, because of the lowering sky, the street lights were on almost everywhere, making a false daylight that gave people's faces a waxy appearance.

Lots of old women. Many old men, too, alone, a marketing basket in their hands. Resignation on their faces. Some stopped from time to time and put their hand to their heart, waiting for a spasm to stop.

Women of all nationalities, carrying young children, a slightly older boy or girl hanging on to their dresses.

"Park here and come with me."

He began with the Pagliatis. There were three customers in the shop and Lucia was very busy.

"My husband's in back. Just push the little door open."

Gino was busy making ravioli on a long marble-topped table covered with flour.

"Oh! Superintendent. . . . I thought you would be coming."

He had a deep voice, a naturally smiling face.

"Is it true that the poor boy is dead?"

That piece of information was not yet in the newspapers.

"Who told you that?"

"A reporter who was here ten minutes ago. He photographed me and I'm going to have my picture in the paper."

"I'd like you to tell me once again what you told me last night, with as much detail as possible. You were coming back from your brother- and sister-in-law's . . ."

"Yes, the one who's expecting a baby. On the Rue de Charonne. We had only taken one umbrella because when

28

we're out on the street, walking, Lucia always takes my arm.

"You remember it was raining hard, a real cloudburst. Several times I thought the umbrella was going to turn inside out and I had to hold it in front of us like a shield.

"That explains why I didn't see him sooner. . . ."

"Who?"

"The murderer. He must have been walking a little way in front of us, but I was only concerned with keeping the rain off us and not stepping in the puddles. Or he might have been standing in a doorway. . . ."

"When you did see him?"

"He had already got farther than the café, Chez Jules, which was still lit up."

"Could you see how he was dressed?"

"I talked that over with my wife last evening. We both think he was wearing a light-colored raincoat, with a belt. He walked with an easy step, very quickly."

"Did he look as if he was following the young man in the jacket?"

"He was walking quicker than he was, as if he wanted to catch up with him, or to pass him."

"How far were you from the two men?"

"A hundred yards, perhaps. I could show you."

"Did the man in front turn around?"

"No. The other man caught up with him. I saw his arm rise and fall. I didn't see the knife. He struck three or four times and the young man in the jacket fell on his face on the sidewalk. The killer took several steps toward the Rue du Chemin-Vert, then he turned back. He must have seen us, because we were then only about sixty yards away. But even so he bent over and struck again two or three times. . . ."

"You didn't run after him?"

"Well, you see, I'm rather fat and I have high blood pressure. I can't run easily."

He had reddened, embarrassed.

"We walked more quickly while we went around the corner this time."

"Did you hear a car start up?"

"I don't think so. . . . I didn't think of that."

Mechanically, without Maigret's having had to tell him, Janvier was taking the interview down in shorthand.

"When you got up to the wounded man, what then?"

"You saw him exactly as I left him. His jacket was torn in several places and the blood was pouring out. I thought at once of getting a doctor and I ran to Monsieur Pardon's, telling Lucia to stay there."

"Why?"

"I don't know. I felt he shouldn't be left alone."

"Did your wife have anything to tell you when you got back?"

"No one had come by, almost as if it were on purpose."

"The wounded man didn't speak?"

"No. He was having trouble breathing, gurgling in his chest. Lucia will tell you the same. It's her busy time, just now."

"Is there any other detail that comes to mind?"

"No, none. I've told you everything I know."

"Thank you, Gino."

"How is Madame Maigret?"

"Very well, thank you."

A passage at the side led to a little courtyard where a welder was working in his glass-fronted workshop. There were courtyards and blind alleys like that scattered throughout the district. There were craftsmen in all of them.

They crossed the street and a little farther on Maigret

pushed open the door of Chez Jules. The little café was almost as dark in the daylight as it was at night, and the opaque white globe was lit. A heavily built man with his shirt sticking out between his trousers and his vest was standing at the counter. He had a red face, a thick neck, and a double chin that looked like a goiter.

"What can I get you, Monsieur Maigret? A little glass of Sancerre? It comes from my cousin. He . . ."

"Two glasses," Maigret said, standing at the counter himself.

"You're not the first today."

"There was a reporter, I know."

"He took my picture, just as I am just now, holding a bottle. You know Lebon. He worked on the roads for thirty years. Then he had an accident and now he gets a pension plus a small compensation for his eye. He was here last evening."

"There were four of you playing cards, weren't there?"

"Auction *manille*. Always the same players, every evening except Sunday. I close on Sundays."

"Are you married?"

"My wife is upstairs. She's an invalid."

"What time did the young man come in?"

"It must have been ten o'clock."

Maigret glanced at the clock, complete with advertisement, which hung on the wall.

"Don't pay any attention to that. It's twenty minutes fast. . . . First he pushed the door open a few inches, as if he wanted to see what kind of place it was. The card game was noisy—the butcher was winning and when he wins he gets insulting, as if he were the only one who could play . . ."

"He came in. And then what?"

"I asked him from my place at the card table what he

31

wanted to drink. He hesitated a bit, then mumbled: 'Do you have any brandy?'

"I waited until I'd played the four cards I had left in my hand and went behind the counter. While I was serving him I noticed the triangular black box he was wearing on his chest, hanging from a strap around his neck, and I thought it must be a camera. Some tourists do get lost around here, but not very often.

"I went back to my place at the table. Baboeuf had dealt the cards. The young man didn't seem in a hurry. He wasn't interested in the game either. . . ."

"Did he seem preoccupied?"

"No."

"He wasn't standing facing the door as if he was waiting for someone?"

"I didn't notice anything."

"Or as if he was afraid someone might come in?"

"No. He stood there, one elbow on the counter, and from time to time he touched his lips to the glass."

"What did you think of him?"

"Well, he was soaking wet, you know. He looked just like a lot of young people these days, with his jacket and his long hair.

"We went on playing cards as if he wasn't there. Baboeuf got more and more excited because he kept on getting all the good cards.

" 'You'd better go home and see what your wife's up to,' Lebon joked.

" 'You go and check on yours. She's a bit too young for you, she . . .'

"I thought for a moment they were going to hit each other. Then it calmed down, as it always does. Baboeuf played the ace.

" 'What do you say to that?'

32

"Then Lebon, who was sitting beside me on the bench, gave me a dig in the ribs with his elbow and I looked at the customer standing at the bar. I looked at him but I didn't understand. He looked as if he was laughing at a private joke, isn't that so, François? I wondered what you were trying to show me. You whispered: 'I'll tell you later.'"

And the man with the blind eye took up the story.

"I had noticed a movement of his hand on the machine. I have a nephew who got a thing like that for Christmas and he amuses himself by recording what his parents say. He looked so angelic, standing there with his drink, but he was listening to everything we were saying, and it was all going on the tape."

"I wonder what he hoped to gain by that," grumbled Jules.

"Nothing. Like my nephew . . . He records for the fun of recording, then he forgets all about it. Once he let his parents hear one of their rows and my brother almost broke the tape recorder:

"'If I catch you at it again, you little bastard . . .'

"Baboeuf would have been furious too if he'd heard the things he said last night."

"How long did the boy stay?"

"A bit less than half an hour."

"Did he have only one drink?"

"Yes. He even left a little cognac in the bottom of his glass."

"He went out and you didn't hear anything after that?"

"Not a thing. Only the wind, and the water gushing from the drainpipe onto the pavement."

"No other customer came in before him?"

"You see, I only stay open in the evenings for the card game, because only the regulars come. There's never a lot

of people except in the morning for their coffee and croissants, or a Vichy water. About ten o'clock or ten thirty
workmen come in for a break, when there's some work
going on anywhere nearby. I'm busiest when people come
to have a drink before lunch or before dinner."

"Thank you."

Here too Janvier had taken the interview down in
shorthand and the proprietor had kept on looking at him
as he did it.

"He's told me nothing new," Maigret sighed. "He has
only confirmed what I knew already."

They got into the car again. Some women were watching them, for their identity was known already.

"Where to, Chief?"

"Back to the office first."

His two visits to the Rue Popincourt had not been useless. Above all, he had the story of the attack, from the
Neapolitan. Antoine Batille's assailant had first stabbed
him several times. He had begun to move away when, for
some unknown reason, he had turned back on his tracks,
in spite of the couple a short distance away on the sidewalk. Was it in order to finish off his victim that he had
stabbed again before running off?

He had been wearing a light-colored, belted raincoat,
that was all anyone knew about him. As soon as he was
back at the Quai des Orfèvres, Maigret, in his office,
which was agreeably warm, telephoned the Pagliatis' shop.

"May I speak to your husband for a moment? This is
Maigret speaking."

"I'll call him, Superintendent."

And Gino's voice:

"Hello, what is it?"

"Tell me, there's one thing I forgot to ask you. Was the
killer wearing a hat?"

34

"A reporter has just asked me the same thing. He's the third since this morning. I had to ask my wife. She can't swear to it, but she's almost sure he was wearing a dark-colored hat. It happened so quickly, you see . . ."

The light-colored, belted raincoat seemed to point to a fairly young man, while the hat would probably mean he was a few years older. In fact, few young people wear a hat these days.

"Tell me, Janvier, do you understand tape recorders?"

Maigret knew nothing about them, nor did he know anything about photography or about cars, which was why it was his wife who drove. It took all his mechanical knowledge to turn the television from one channel to another in the evenings.

"My son has one just like that."

"Take care not to erase the recording."

"Don't worry, Chief."

Janvier smiled and pressed some buttons. They could hear a confused noise, the sound of forks and plates and indistinct voices in the distance.

"And what will Madame have?"

"Do you have any top round?"

"Of course, Madame."

"I'll have that with plenty of onions and gherkins."

"Remember what the doctor told you. No vinegar."

"A minute steak and a top round with plenty of onions and gherkins. Would you like the salad served with it?"

The recording was far from perfect and there was a continuous background noise that made it impossible to distinguish the words clearly.

A silence, then a sigh, very distinct.

"You'll always be irresponsible. You're going to have to get up tonight too to take bicarbonate of soda."

"It's I who get up and not you. Anyway, since you go on snoring whatever happens . . ."

"I don't snore."

"You do snore, particularly when you've drunk too much beaujolais, as you're about to do now. . . ."

"One steak done to a turn. I'll bring the top round in one moment."

"You hardly touch it, at home."

"We aren't at home."

There was a gurgling sound. A voice called: "Waiter! Waiter! When you decide to pay some attention to us . . ."

Then silence, as if the tape had been cut off. Then a toneless voice spoke very clearly, since this time it must have been speaking directly into the microphone. "The Brasserie Lorraine, on the Boulevard Beaumarchais."

Almost certainly the voice of Antoine Batille, noting in that way where the recording had been made. He had obviously had dinner on the Boulevard Beaumarchais and had switched on his tape recorder. The waiter would probably remember him. It was easy to check.

"You can go over there in a minute," Maigret said. "Turn the thing on again."

Some curious sounds at first, street noises, because they could hear the cars going by. Maigret wondered for a time what the boy had been trying to record, and it took him a while to realize that it was the noises of water in drains and gutters. The sound was difficult to identify, but it changed suddenly and they were once more in a public place, a café or a bar, where there was quite a bit of noise.

"What did he tell you?"

"That it was O.K."

The voices were thick, but still quite clear.

"Did you go there, Mimile?"

"Lucien and Gouvion are taking turns. In this weather . . ."

"What kind of car is it?"

"Same as usual."

"Don't you think it's a bit too close?"

"Too close to what?"

"Too close to Paris."

"Seeing he only goes there on Fridays . . ."

The sound of glasses, of cups, of more voices. Silence.

"Recorded at the Café des Amis, Place de la Bastille."

It was not far from the Boulevard Beaumarchais, not far from the Rue Popincourt either. Batille didn't hang around, doubtless so as not to be noticed, and he set off in the rain for a new place.

"And what about your own wife? It's easy to talk about others, but you'd do well to keep an eye on what goes on in your own home."

That must be the butcher, the game of cards in Chez Jules.

"Don't you worry about my affairs, I'm giving you some good advice. It's not because you're winning . . ."

"I'm winning because I don't throw away my trumps like a fool."

"Stop it, you two."

"He's the one who started . . ."

If the voices had been shriller, one would have thought it was a children's quarrel.

"Shall we get on with the game?"

"I don't play with anyone who . . ."

"He was just talking off the top of his head. He didn't mean anyone in particular."

"Let him say so, then, if that's how it was."

A silence.

"You see, he's careful to keep his mouth shut."

"I'm keeping it shut because this is so stupid. And here, I'm leading my ace. That fixes you, doesn't it?"

The sound was poor. The people talking were too far away from the microphone, and Janvier had to play that piece of tape three times. Each time they made out one or two more words.

Batille finally said: "Chez Jules, a small local bistrot, Rue Popincourt."

"Is that all?"

"That's all."

The rest of the tape was blank. Batille must have spoken the last words on the sidewalk a few seconds before being attacked by an unknown man.

"What about the other two cassettes?"

"They are blank. They're still in their original wrappings. He intended to use them later in the evening, I suppose."

"Did anything strike you as odd?"

"The voices at the Place de la Bastille?"

"Yes. Play that bit again."

Janvier took it down in shorthand. Then he replayed the few bits of dialogue which seemed, the more they heard them, to take on a more and more particular meaning.

"I would say there were at least three of them."

"Yes."

"Plus the two they talked about, Gouvion and Lucien. A little more than half an hour after that was recorded, Antoine was attacked on the Rue Popincourt."

"But the man didn't take his tape recorder."

"Perhaps because the Pagliatis were getting close."

"I forgot one thing on the Rue Popincourt. Last evening I caught sight of an old woman at a first-floor window, almost opposite the spot where the boy was attacked."

"I understand, Chief. Shall I go there right now?"

Maigret, left on his own, went and stood in front of the window. The Batilles must have been to the hospital and the forensic surgeon would soon have the body.

Maigret had not yet seen the dead boy's sister, the girl the family called Minou, who had, so it seemed, some very odd friends.

Strings of barges glided slowly along the gray Seine and the tugs lowered their funnels as they passed under the Pont Saint-Michel.

Throughout the cold season the terrace was protected by glass screens and heated by two braziers. The room, around the horseshoe-shaped bar, was fairly big, the tables tiny, the chairs the kind that could be stacked at night.

Maigret sat down near a pillar and, when one of the waiters came by, ordered a beer. He gazed at the faces around him with an absent expression. The clientele was mixed. At the bar, for example, there were mainly men in blue work-clothes or old men from the surrounding district who came in for their glass of red wine.

As for the others, those who were sitting down, they were of all kinds: a woman in black surrounded by her two children and a large suitcase, as if she were in a station waiting room; a couple holding hands and gazing rapturously into each other's eyes; some very long-haired boys who snickered as they followed the waitress with their eyes and teased her every time she passed near them.

For, besides the two waiters, there was a waitress with a particularly unpleasant face. In her black dress and white apron she was thin, stooped with tiredness, and it was with difficulty that she managed to direct vague smiles at the customers.

Some men and women were quite well dressed, others less so. Some were eating sandwiches and drinking coffee or a glass of beer. Others were having an apéritif.

The proprietor sat at the cash desk, dressed in black with a white shirt and a black tie, his brown hair carefully plastered over the baldness which it covered with an inadequate network of fine dark lines.

It was his post, one could tell that, and nothing that went on in his establishment escaped him. He watched the two waiters coming and going, at the same time keeping an eye on the boy who put the bottles and glasses on the trays. Each time he was given a token he pressed a key on the cash register and a figure appeared in the little glass aperture.

He had obviously been in the business a long time, and he had probably begun as a waiter himself. Maigret was to discover later, when he went downstairs to the washroom, that there was another, smaller, low-ceilinged room below, where some customers were eating.

This was not a place where one played cards, or dominoes. It was a place for birds of passage, and there must have been very few regulars. Those who remained seated at the tables for any length of time were waiting to keep an appointment nearby.

Maigret finally rose and went over to the cash desk, under no illusions as to the welcome he would get.

"Excuse me, Monsieur."

He held his badge out discreetly in the palm of his hand.

"Superintendent Maigret, of the Criminal Police."

The proprietor's eyes kept their distrustful expression,

the same look he had for the waiters and for the customers who came and went.

"So?"

"Were you here last evening at about nine thirty?"

"I was in bed. My wife takes the desk in the evenings."

"Were the same waiters on duty?"

He continued to keep a watchful eye on them.

"Yes."

"I'd like to ask them two or three questions about some customers they may have noticed."

The black eyes stared at him, hardly encouraging.

"We only let respectable people in here and the waiters are very busy just now."

"I only need a minute with each one. Was the waitress here too?"

"No. There's less of a crowd in the evenings. Jérôme!"

One of the waiters stopped abruptly in front of the desk, tray in hand. The proprietor turned to Maigret.

"Go on. Ask your questions."

"Did you notice, last evening, about nine thirty, a young man, about twenty-one, wearing a brown jacket, with a tape recorder hanging around his neck?"

The waiter turned toward the proprietor, then toward Maigret, and shook his head.

"Do you know any regular customer nicknamed Mimile?"

"No."

When it was the second waiter's turn the results were no more spectacular. They hesitated to answer, as if they were afraid of their boss, and it was difficult to know whether they were telling the truth. Maigret, disappointed, returned to his table and ordered another glass of beer. It was at that moment that he went downstairs to the washroom and discovered a third waiter below, younger than the two upstairs.

He decided to sit down and order a drink.

"Tell me, do you ever work upstairs?"

"Three days out of four. We all take a turn at being down here."

"Last evening?"

"I was up there."

"At night too? About half past nine?"

"Right up till we closed, at eleven. We closed early because, what with the weather, there was hardly anyone here."

"Did you see a young man with fairly long hair, wearing a suède jacket, with a tape recorder hanging around his neck?"

"So it was a tape recorder."

"You saw it?"

"Yes. It isn't the tourist season yet. I thought it was a camera like the ones Americans carry. Then there was the matter of a customer."

"What customer?"

"There were three of them at the next table. When the young man left, one of them watched him go with a worried, anxious look. He called me over.

" 'Tell me, Toto . . .'

"Of course my name isn't Toto, but it's a way of speaking some people have, especially around here.

" 'What did the fellow have to drink?'

" 'A brandy.'

" 'You didn't see if he used the thing he was carrying?'

" 'I didn't see him take any pictures.'

" 'Pictures my eye! It was a tape recorder, idiot. Have you ever seen that fellow before?'

" 'This is the first time.'

42

" 'What about me?'

" 'I think I've served you three or four times before.'

" 'That's all right, then. Give us the same again.' "

The waiter moved off, because a customer was tapping his table with a coin to attract his attention. The customer paid. The waiter gave him his change and helped him on with his coat.

Then he came right back to Maigret.

"You said there were three of them."

"Yes. The one who spoke to me and who seemed the most important is a man of about thirty-five, built like a physical-training instructor, brown hair, dark eyes with bushy eyebrows."

"Had he really been in only two or three times before?"

"I only noticed him those times."

"What about the others?"

"One of them, a redhead with a scar, hangs around this district quite a lot, and he comes in and has a glass of rum at the counter."

"And the third?"

"I've heard him called Mimile by his pals. I know him by sight and I know where he lives. He's a picture framer. His shop is on the Faubourg Saint-Antoine, almost at the corner of the Rue Trousseau. That's where I live, the Rue Trousseau."

"Does he come in here a lot?"

"I've seen him a few times. Not very often."

"With the two others?"

"No. With a little blonde who seems to come from around here too, a salesgirl or something like that."

"Thank you. You can't think of anything else to tell me?"

"No. If I think of anything, or if I see them again . . ."

"In that case, telephone me at Criminal Police. Ask for

me or, if I'm not there, for one of my assistants. What's your name?"

"Julien. Julien Blond. The others call me Blondinet, because I'm the youngest. When I'm as old as they are, I hope I'll have a better job than this."

Maigret was too near home to go and have lunch at the Brasserie Dauphine. He almost regretted it. He would have liked to take Janvier there and brief him on what he had just found out.

"Have you got anywhere?" his wife asked.

"I don't know if it's anything worth while. I have to look everywhere."

At two o'clock he gathered together three of his favorite inspectors in his office—Janvier, Lucas, and young Lapointe, who would no doubt still be called that when he was fifty.

"Would you play the tape again, Janvier? You two, listen carefully."

Lucas and Lapointe pricked up their ears, of course, as soon as the piece recorded at the Café des Amis began.

"I went there a little while ago. I know the profession and the address of one of the three men seated around the table speaking in low voices. The one they call Mimile. He's a picture framer with a shop on the Faubourg Saint-Antoine, two or three houses before you get to the Rue Trousseau."

Maigret didn't dare feel too pleased. Things had gone a bit too quickly for his liking.

"You two will take up a position near the picture framer's shop. Arrange for two of your colleagues to relieve you this evening. If Mimile goes out, one of you must follow him, preferably both of you. If he meets someone, one of you stick to him. The same thing if someone who doesn't look like a customer comes to the shop. In other

44

words, I want to know the people he may be in contact with."

"That's understood, Chief."

"You, Janvier, will look through the files for men of about thirty-five, well built, good-looking, brown hair, thick eyebrows, and black eyes. There must be several, but it's someone who doesn't hide himself, perhaps someone who has never been sentenced or someone who has done his time."

When he was alone in his office he rang the Forensic Institute. Doctor Desalle came to the telephone.

"Maigret here. Have you finished the autopsy, Doctor?"

"Half an hour ago. Do you know how many stab wounds that boy had? Seven. All in the back. All about the level of the heart, and yet the heart was not touched."

"What about the knife?"

"I was coming to that. The blade is not wide but long and pointed. In my opinion it's one of those Swedish switchblade knives where the blade shoots out when a button is pressed.

"Only one of the wounds was fatal, the one that perforated the right lung and caused a fatal hemorrhage."

"Did you notice anything else?"

"The boy was healthy, well built, not very athletic—the type of intellectual who doesn't take enough exercise. All the other organs were in excellent condition. Although his blood contained a certain amount of alcohol, he was not drunk. He had had two or three glasses of what I think must have been brandy."

"Thank you, Doctor."

"You'll get my report tomorrow morning."

There was still the routine work to be done. The Public Prosecutor had appointed an examining magistrate, Monsieur Poiret, with whom Maigret had never worked.

Another young man. It seemed to the superintendent that for several years the legal profession had been renewing itself with disconcerting rapidity. Wasn't that impression due to his own age?

He telephoned the examining magistrate, who asked him to come up at once if he was free. He took with him the transcripts of the tape-recorded conversations which Janvier had typed out.

Poiret only merited one of the old offices as yet. Maigret sat down on an uncomfortable chair.

"I'm happy to meet you," the magistrate said pleasantly. He was a tall man with his fair hair crew cut.

"And I you, Monsieur. Of course I'm here to talk to you about young Batille."

The magistrate unfolded an afternoon paper where a three-column headline sprawled on the first page. There was a photograph of a young man, his hair not yet grown long, who looked very much a "boy of good family."

"I understand you have seen the father and mother."

"Yes, it was I who broke the news to them. They had just come back from the theater, both of them in evening dress. I think they were humming a tune as they came through the front door. I have rarely seen two people collapse so completely so quickly."

"Was he an only child?"

"No, there's a sister, a girl of eighteen, who seems to be rather a handful."

"Have you seen her?"

"Not yet."

"What is their apartment like?"

"Very big, luxurious, but bright and gay. A few antiques, but not many. The whole feeling is modern, but not aggressively so."

"They must be very rich," sighed the magistrate.

"I suppose so."

"The paper has an account of what happened which seems to me to be highly romanticized."

"Does it mention the tape recorder?"

"No. Why? Does a tape recorder play an important part?"

"Perhaps. I'm not sure yet. Antoine Batille had a passion for recording conversations on the street, in restaurants, in cafés. For him, they were human documents. He led a rather lonely life and he often went out on the hunt like that, particularly in the evenings and especially in the poorer districts.

"Last night he began in a restaurant on the Boulevard Beaumarchais, where he recorded snatches of a domestic quarrel.

"Then he went to a café on the Place de la Bastille and here is the text of his recording."

He held the paper out to the magistrate, who frowned.

"That seems fairly incriminating, doesn't it?"

"It's obviously about a rendezvous for Thursday evening in front of a house near Paris. Certainly a weekend place, for the owner only comes on Fridays and leaves on Monday mornings."

"That is indeed what the text says."

"In order to be sure that the villa is empty, the gang has it watched by two men who relieve each other. I know from another source who Mimile is and I have his address."

"In that case?"

The magistrate seemed to be saying that it was all tied up, but the superintendent was less optimistic.

"If it's the gang I have in mind . . ." he began. "In the last two years several important villas have been robbed while their owners were in Paris. In almost every case the stolen objects were pictures and valuable curios. At Tessancourt they left behind two canvases that were only copies, which indicates . . ."

"People who know about art."

"One person who does, at least."

"What's worrying you?"

"That those people have never yet killed anyone. It's not their line."

"But it could happen, in a case like yesterday evening."

"Let's suppose that they suddenly had suspicions that the tape recorder was working. It would be easy for two of them, let's say, to follow Antoine Batille. Once he was in a deserted street, like the Rue Popincourt, all they had to do was jump on him and grab his tape recorder."

The magistrate sighed regretfully.

"Of course."

"Thieves like that rarely kill, and when they do it's in desperate circumstances. They have operated for two years without being caught. We haven't the slightest idea how they resell the pictures and *objets d'art*. That supposes at least one brain behind them, a man who knows about painting, who has contacts, who plans the raids, who may even take part in them himself after he has allotted a specific task to each one.

"That man, who most certainly exists, does not let his accomplices kill."

"In that case, what do you think?"

"I don't think anything yet. I'm fumbling in the dark. I am following that trail, of course. Two of my inspectors are watching the picture-framing shop kept by the man called Mimile. Still another is going through the files looking for a man of about thirty-five with bushy dark eyebrows."

"You'll keep me informed?"

"As soon as I have anything new."

Could one believe all that Gino Pagliati had said? The Neapolitan had sworn that the killer had struck several times, that he had taken a few steps toward the corner of the street, and that he had come back again and struck three more times.

That did not go with the assumption of a semiprofessional, either, especially when one took into account the fact that he had not taken away the tape recorder.

Janvier gave him a report on his visit to the woman seen at a first-floor window.

"Madame Esparbès, a widow of seventy-two. She lives alone in an apartment of three rooms with kitchen, where she has lived for ten years. Her husband was an officer. She has a pension and lives comfortably but not extravagantly.

"She suffers from nerves and says that she rarely sleeps any more, and she has the habit of peering out of the window every time she wakes up.

" 'It's an old woman's compulsion, Inspector.'

" 'What did you see last evening? Don't be afraid to give details, even if they may seem irrelevant to you.'

" 'I hadn't yet got ready to go to bed. I listened to the ten o'clock news on the radio as usual. Then I turned off the radio and went over to look out of the window. I hadn't seen rain like that for a long time and it brought back memories. . . . That's not important.

" 'At about ten-thirty, or a little before, a young man wearing a jacket came out of the little café opposite and he had what I thought was a rather large camera on his chest. I was a little surprised at that.

" 'At almost the same time I saw another young man . . .'

" 'You're sure it was a young man?'

49

" 'I thought he was quite young, yes. He was smaller than the first man, and a little broader, but not much. I didn't notice where he came from. In a few swift, and doubtless silent, steps he was behind the other man and he began to strike him several times. I almost opened the window and screamed, but it wouldn't have done any good. The victim was on the ground already. Then the killer bent over him, and lifted up his head by the hair, to look at his face.'

" 'Are you sure of that?'

" 'I'm certain. The street lamp isn't far away, and I myself could vaguely make out his features.'

" 'And then what?'

" 'He went away. Then he turned back on his tracks, as if he had forgotten something. The Pagliatis were walking along the sidewalk about fifty yards away, under their umbrella. But the man still struck the one on the ground three more times, then he ran away.'

" 'Did he go around the corner into the Rue du Chemin-Vert?'

" 'Yes. The Pagliatis arrived on the scene then. . . . But you know the rest. I recognized Doctor Pardon. I didn't know the man who was with him.'

" 'Would you recognize the killer?'

" 'Not to make a formal identification. Not his face. Only his figure.'

" 'Are you sure he was young?'

" 'In my opinion he is no more than thirty.'

" 'Long hair?'

" 'No.'

" 'Mustache, sideburns?'

" 'No. I would have noticed that.'

" 'Was he as wet as if he had been walking in the rain, or had he just come out of a house?'

" 'They were both soaking. It took only a few minutes outside for one's clothes to be wringing wet.'

" 'Was he wearing a hat?'

" 'Yes. A dark hat. I think it was brown.'

" 'Thank you.'

" 'I've told you everything I know, but please see that my name doesn't get into the papers. I have nephews in good jobs and they would be upset if people knew I live here. . . .' "

The telephone rang. Maigret recognized Pardon's voice.

"Is that you, Maigret? Am I disturbing you? I didn't expect to find you in your office. I thought I'd call you to see if you have any news."

"We've got a lead, but I don't know if it's any good. As for the autopsy, it confirms your diagnosis. Only one wound was fatal, the one that entered the right lung."

"Do you think it was an underworld killing?"

"I don't know. There weren't many prowlers or drunks about in the streets at that time. There was no fight. Young Batille didn't quarrel with anybody in the two places he was in before he went into Jules's café."

"Thank you. You see, I feel a bit involved in this case. Now, back to work. I have eleven patients in my waiting room."

"Good luck!"

Maigret went over and sat in his armchair, chose a pipe from his desk, and filled it, his gaze as vague as the view from the window, which was becoming more and more foggy.

Chapter **3**   At about five twenty there was a
telephone call from Lucas.

"I thought you'd like me to make a preliminary report,
Chief. I'm in a little bar just opposite the picture framer's
shop. Incidentally, his name is Emile Branchu. He set up
shop on the Rue du Faubourg-Saint-Antoine about two
years ago.

"He seems to have come from Marseilles, but that's not
certain. They say, too, that he was married down there
but that he's separated from his wife, or divorced.

"He lives alone. An old woman, from the neighborhood, comes in to clean for him, and he takes most of his
meals in a restaurant where most of the customers are regulars.

"He has a car, a green 6 CV, which he keeps in the
courtyard nearest his shop. He goes out a lot in the evenings and comes home in the small hours, often with a
pretty girl with him, never the same one twice. Not the
type of girl one finds around here or in the night clubs on
the Rue du Lappe. They look like models and wear evening dresses and fur coats.

"Does that interest you?"

"Of course. Go on."

Of all of his men, Lucas had worked for him the long-
est, and Maigret now called him *"tu."* He called Lapointe
"tu" too, because he had been almost a boy when he
started and still looked like an overgrown schoolboy.

"There have only been three customers, two men and a

52

woman. The woman bought a mirror with a magnifying mirror on one side—he sells mirrors too. One of the men brought a photographic enlargement for framing and took a long time making his choice.

"The third customer went off with a framed picture under his arm. I was able to see it quite clearly, because he went over to the glass door to look at it. It was a landscape with a river, the work of an amateur."

"Has he telephoned anyone?"

"I can see the phone very well from where I'm watching. It's on the counter. He hasn't used it. On the other hand, when the paper boy came past, he came to the door and bought two different newspapers."

"Is Lapointe still there?"

"He's outside at the moment. There's a back door giving on to not only the courtyard but a whole network of alleys, the kind this district is full of. Since there's a car and he might use it, it would be better if Lourtie and Neveu, who are going to relieve us, brought a car with them."

"I'll see to that. Thank you."

Janvier had come downstairs again with about fifteen photographs of brown-haired men with bushy eyebrows, about thirty-five years old.

"These are all I can find, Chief. Do you need me any more? It's the birthday of one of the children. . . ."

"Wish him a happy birthday from me."

Maigret went into the inspectors' office, saw Lourtie, and told him to take a car when he went to the Rue du Faubourg-Saint-Antoine.

"Where is Neveu?"

"He's somewhere in the building. He'll be right back."

Maigret had nothing more to do at the Quai and he went down to the courtyard with the photographs in his pocket. He went through the gateway, saluted the man on duty with a wave of the hand, and went in the direction of the Boulevard du Palais, where he found a taxi. He was not in a bad temper, but he wasn't very happy either. One might have said that he was leading this investigation without conviction, as if something had been wrong from the start, and he kept thinking of the scene that had taken place in the pouring rain on the Rue Popincourt.

Young Batille, who had come out of the dimly lit café where the four men were playing cards. The Pagliatis, under their umbrella, still quite far down the street. Madame Esparbès at her window.

And someone, a man of thirty at the most, who suddenly appeared on the scene. No one could say if he had been waiting in a doorway for Antoine Batille to come out or if he too had been walking along the sidewalk, following him. He covered several yards quickly, then struck once, twice, four times at least.

He heard the footsteps of the pasta-maker and his wife, who were no more than fifty yards away. He went toward the corner of the Rue du Chemin-Vert and, just as he was about to turn the corner, he retraced his steps.

Why did he lean over his victim, and why did he only lift his head? He didn't feel his wrist or his chest, to see if Antoine was dead. He looked at his face.

Was it to reassure himself that it was in fact the man he had decided to attack? From that moment, something was not quite right. Why did he strike the man lying on the ground three more times?

It was a film that Maigret ran over and over again in his head, as if he hoped to understand all of a sudden.

"Place de la Bastille," he said to the taxi driver.

The proprietor of the Café des Amis was still at the cash desk, his hair plastered over his bald pate. Their eyes met, and the expression in those of the proprietor was not welcoming. Instead of taking a seat upstairs, Maigret went down to the basement, where he took a seat at a table. There were many more people than in the morning. It was the time for the before-dinner apéritif. When the waiter came to take his order, he was less friendly than before.

"A beer."

And, holding the pack of photographs out to him:

"See if you recognize any of these men."

"I haven't got much time."

"It'll only take a minute."

The proprietor must have had a word with him when he saw the superintendent come up from the basement after having spent some time there.

The waiter hesitated, then finally took the photographs.

"I'd better take them over in the corner to look at them."

He came back almost at once and handed the bundle back to Maigret.

"I don't recognize anyone."

He appeared to be sincere and he went to get the beer Maigret had ordered. There was nothing left for Maigret to do but go home for dinner. He took his time drinking his beer, then climbed the stairs to the street floor and saw Lapointe sitting alone at a table just opposite him.

Lapointe saw him too, but pretended not to recognize him. Emile Branchu must have been somewhere in the café, and the superintendent made an effort not to look too hard at the customers.

He had two hundred yards to go to reach home, where there was a pervading aroma of baked mackerel. Madame Maigret cooked them in white wine, in a slow oven, with lots of mustard.

She saw immediately that he was not happy with his case and asked no questions.

When they were at the table, she remarked:

"Don't you want the television?"

It had become a habit, a compulsion.

"On the seven o'clock news they talked about Antoine Batille for a long time. They went to the Sorbonne to interview several of his friends."

"What did they have to say about him?"

"That he was a nice boy, rather retiring, a bit embarrassed to belong to such a well-known family. He had a passion for tape recorders and he was waiting for a miniature one that can be held in the palm of the hand to arrive from Japan."

"Is that all?"

"They tried to question his sister. All she said was 'I have nothing to say.'

" 'Where were you that night?'

" 'At Saint-Germain-des-Prés.'

" 'Did you get on well with your brother?'

" 'He left me alone and I left him alone.' "

The reporters were all over the place, on the Rue Popincourt, at the Quai d'Anjou, at the Sorbonne. Even the provincial radio stations had got hold of it. They already had a label for the case: *The Madman of the Rue Popincourt*.

They dwelt on the number of stab wounds—seven! In two groups! The murderer had retraced his steps to strike again, as if he had not reached his quota.

"Does that not suggest the idea of a revenge killing?" one of the reporters insinuated. "If the seven blows had been struck one after another, one could believe in a kind of mad rage, more or less unconscious. A large number of blows, which always impresses the jury, is almost always

56

the sign that a murderer has lost control of himself. Batille's killer was interrupted, went away, came back on his tracks to strike the last three blows."

One of the papers finished up with:

"Did the tape recorder play a part in this case? We believe that the police attach a certain importance to it, but no one at the Quai des Orfèvres is willing to answer questions on the subject."

At eight thirty the telephone rang.

"Neveu here, Chief. Lucas told me to keep you informed."

"Where are you?"

"In the little bar opposite the picture framer's shop. Before Lourtie and I arrived, Emile Branchu shut up shop and went to the Place de la Bastille, where he had a drink. As he passed by the cash desk he greeted the proprietor, who returned his greeting as if he were a regular.

"The picture framer didn't speak to anyone. He read the newspapers he had in his pocket. Lapointe was there. . . ."

"I saw him."

"Good. Did you also know that he went and had his dinner in a little restaurant where his napkin is kept in a pigeonhole and where they call him Monsieur Emile?"

"I didn't know that."

"Lapointe says he ate very well there. It seems that the blood sausage . . ."

"Then what?"

"Branchu went home, pulled down the shop shutter, and fixed the wooden panel to the glass door. A faint light is showing through the window shutters. Lourtie is watching the courtyard."

"Do you have the car?"

"It's parked a few yards from here."

The first channel was rife with torch singers of both sexes. Maigret hated that. There was an old American film, with Gary Cooper, which Maigret and his wife watched, on the second channel.

The film finished at a quarter to eleven and Maigret was in shirt sleeves, brushing his teeth, when the telephone rang again. This time it was Lourtie.

"Where are you?" the superintendent asked him.

"On the Rue Fontaine. The picture framer went out at about half past ten and got his car from the courtyard. Neveu and I took the police car."

"Did he notice you following him?"

"I don't think so. He came directly here, as if it was an old habit, and after he had found a parking place he went into the Pink Rabbit."

"What is the Pink Rabbit?"

"A striptease club. The doorman greeted him as if he knew him. We went in after him, Neveu and I, because two men are less noticeable than one in places like that. Neveu even acted the part of someone a little drunk."

That was Neveu all over. He loved adding the personal touch. He also liked putting on disguises, which he carried out to the smallest detail.

"Our man is at the bar. He shook hands with the bartender. The proprietor, a small fat man in a dinner jacket, came over and shook hands too, and two or three of the girls kissed him."

"The bartender?"

"Correct. He looks very like the description we were given. Between thirty and forty, handsome, Mediterranean type."

When he left the Café des Amis Maigret should have given the pack of photographs to Lucas, who was still on the Rue du Faubourg-Saint-Antoine and would have handed them over to Lourtie. He had thought of it when he left the Quaï des Orfèvres, then it had slipped his mind.

"Go back to the Pink Rabbit. I'll be there in about twenty minutes. What's the name of the bistrot you're calling from?"

"You can't miss it. It's the tobacco shop on the corner. I didn't want to call from the club in case I was overheard."

"Be at the tobacco shop in twenty minutes."

Madame Maigret had understood and, sighing, went to get her husband's hat and coat.

"Shall I call a taxi?"

"Yes, please."

"Will you be long?"

"Less than an hour."

In spite of the fact that they had had a car—which Maigret had never driven—for a year, Madame Maigret preferred to use it as little as possible in Paris. They used it mainly on Saturday evenings and Sunday mornings, to get to Meung-sur-Loire, where they had their little cottage.

"When I retire . . ."

Sometimes it seemed as if Maigret, desperate to retire, was counting the days. At others one could sense that he had a feeling of panic at the idea of leaving the Quai des Orfevres.

Up until three months before, the retiring age for superintendents was sixty-five, and he was sixty-three. A new regulation had changed everything and put the retiring age back to sixty-eight.

In some streets the fog was thicker than in others and the cars moved slowly, their headlights looking as if haloed.

"I've driven you before, haven't I?"

"It's very likely."

"It's funny. I never manage to put a name to your face. I know you're someone well known. Are you an actor?"

"No."

"Have you never been in pictures?"

"No."

"And I haven't seen you on television either?"

Fortunately, they reached the Rue Fontaine at that point.

"Try to find a place to park and wait for me."

"Will you be long?"

"A few minutes."

"That's all right then, because it's just now that the theaters are coming out, and . . ."

Maigret pushed open the door of the tobacco shop and found Lourtie at the counter. He ordered a brandy, since there had been a lot of talk about brandies the previous evening, then he took the photographs out of his pocket and slipped them into the inspector's hand.

"Go to the washroom to look at them, it's safer."

A few moments later Lourtie returned and gave the photographs back to the superintendent.

"It's the one on top of the pile. I've put a cross on the back."

"You're absolutely sure?"

"Absolutely. Except that on the photograph he's three or four years younger. He's still a good-looking man."

"You go back there."

"The strip show is about to begin. You know, we've had to order champagne. They don't serve anything else."

"That's all right. And if anything else of importance happens, particularly if the picture framer goes out of the city, be sure to call me."

Back in the taxi, he looked at the photograph marked

with a cross. It was the best-looking man of the lot. There was something impudent, something sarcastic in his expression. A tough, like the members of the Corsican gang or the gang from Marseilles.

Maigret slept fitfully and was in his office long before nine o'clock. He sent Janvier to Records.

"It came off, then? I didn't dare hope too much. The description was pretty vague."

Janvier came down again a quarter of an hour later with a card.

"*Mila,* Julien Joseph François, born in Marseilles. Bartender by profession. Bachelor. Height . . ."

There followed the various measurements of the said Mila, whose last known domicile was a furnished room on the Rue Notre-Dame-de-Lorette.

Sentenced four years previously to two years' imprisonment for armed robbery. That had taken place at the entrance to a factory in Puteaux. The bank messenger had been able to spring the catch on his case, from which a cloud of thick smoke then appeared. A policeman standing at the corner saw it. A chase. The thieves' car had ended up against a lamppost.

Mila had got himself out of it rather well, first of all because he had claimed to be only an accomplice, then because the thieves had only used toy guns.

Maigret sighed. He knew professional criminals well, but he had never been greatly interested in them. For him, all that was routine, a sort of game that had its rules, sometimes also its pretenses and trickery.

Could one suppose that a man who had used a toy pistol to stage a holdup had twice leapt on a young man, for the sole reason that the man might have recorded snatches of an incriminating conversation? And that when the young man was on the ground, the killer would not have taken the trouble to take his tape recorder away or to break it?

"Hello? Get me Monsieur Poiret, the magistrate, please. . . . Hello, yes. . . . Thank you. Monsieur Poiret? . . . Maigret here. . . . I have some information that raises a few questions and I would like to show it to you. . . . In half an hour? Thank you. . . . I'll be in your office in half an hour."

The sun broke through suddenly. One could almost believe that spring intended to keep its appointment on the 21st. Maigret, with Mila's photograph in his pocket, went off to the director's office for the briefing.

It was a day of comings and goings, of telephone calls. The little gang, of whom only Mila and the picture framer, and a third, unidentified person were known, was apparently planning a robbery in a country house near Paris.

But the Criminal Police of the Quai des Orfèvres were powerless outside the boundaries of Paris. It was the domain of the Criminal Investigation Department, on the Rue des Saussaies, and, in agreement with the magistrate, Maigret telephoned the man whom it was now fashionable to call his homologue.

It was Superintendent Grosjean, a man of long service who was about the same age as Maigret and who, like him, always had a pipe in his mouth. He was a native of Cantal and had kept the flavorful accent of that region.

They met a little later in the enormous buildings of the Rue des Saussaies, which the men of the Criminal Police called "the factory."

After half an hour of work Grosjean got up, grumbling:

"Still, I'll have to make the gesture of referring it to my chief."

When Maigret got back to his office, everything was fixed. It was not necessarily the way he would have liked, but the way that Criminal Investigation was accustomed to work.

"And now what?" Janvier, who had remained in contact with the men on watch on the Rue du Faubourg-Saint-Antoine, asked him.

"A scene right out of a film!"

"Lucas and Marette are on the Rue du Faubourg-Saint-Antoine. Emile came and took his apéritif in the bar they were in, without paying any attention to them. Then he had dinner in the same restaurant as last evening.

"No comings and goings. Two or three customers who looked like genuine customers. There is a little workshop that joins on to the shop and that's where he works."

At about four o'clock Maigret had to go up to the magistrate's to brief him on the plan that had been decided on. When he came down again he was handed a slip of paper on which a name only was written: Monique Batille. The space intended for the purpose of the visit had not been filled in.

How had she got the nickname Minou from Monique? He went toward the waiting room, saw a tall, thin girl wearing black trousers and a trench coat over a transparent blouse.

"You're Superintendent Maigret, aren't you?"

She seemed to be inspecting him from head to foot to reassure herself that he lived up to his reputation.

"Would you care to come with me?"

She went without the slightest embarrassment into the office where so many destinies had been played out. She didn't seem to take any notice of the place and remained detached, taking a packet of Gitanes from her pocket.

"May I smoke?"

A little laugh.

"I forgot that you smoke your pipe all day."

She walked over to the window.

"It's like at home. You can see the Seine. Don't you find it boring?"

Did she want a movable backdrop?

Ah! She let herself sink finally into the armchair while Maigret remained standing by his desk.

"You must be wondering what I have come here for. Don't worry, I'm not here out of idle curiosity. . . . It's true that although I know all kinds of celebrities I've never met any policeman before."

There was no point in trying to stop her. Was it a mannerism she put on to hide a basic shyness?

"Yesterday I waited for you to come and question my parents again, to question me, then the servants, and all that. . . . Isn't that what you usually do? This morning I decided I would come and see you this afternoon. I gave it a lot of thought."

She saw the flicker of a smile on Maigret's lips and guessed what he was thinking.

"I do think quite a bit, believe me. I only talk in this flighty way. My brother's body was found on the Rue Popincourt, wasn't it? It isn't a dreadful street, is it?"

"What do you mean by a dreadful street?"

"A street where criminals meet in the bars and plan their crimes, I don't know, I . . ."

"No. It's just an ordinary street where ordinary people live."

"That's what I thought. Well, my brother went to other places to do his recording, really dangerous places. Once I begged him to take me with him.

64

" 'I can't do it, my child. Where I'm going, you wouldn't be safe. Even I'm not safe there, either.'

"I asked him: 'Do you mean there are criminals there?'

" 'Certainly. Do you know how many bodies are fished out of the Canal Saint-Martin every year?'

"I don't think he was trying to frighten me or to get rid of me. I begged him and begged him. I came back to the subject several times, but he would never take me on any of what he called his expeditions."

Maigret looked at her, surprised that she had retained such freshness beneath a deliberately sophisticated exterior. And her brother seemed to have been, like her, basically only an overgrown child.

"Did he keep his recordings?"

"There are dozens of cassettes in his room, carefully numbered, the numbers corresponding to a catalogue that he kept up to date."

"No one has touched it since . . . since his death?"

"No."

"Is the body at home?"

"They've turned the small drawing room, which we call Mother's drawing room, into a mortuary chapel, with candles. The other drawing room was too big. There are black hangings at the door of the apartment, too. It's all too gloomy. They shouldn't do things like that any more these days, don't you think?"

"What else were you going to tell me?"

"Nothing. That he ran risks. That he met people of all kinds. I don't know if he spoke to them, or if he got to know any of those people. . . ."

"Did he ever carry a gun?"

"It's funny you should ask that."

"Why?"

"He managed to persuade Daddy to give him one of his

65

revolvers. He kept it in his room. And he said to me, not very long ago:

" 'I'll be glad when I'm twenty-one. I shall ask for a permit to carry a gun. Given the type of research I do . . .' "

That lent a new pathos, and an almost unreal character, to the scene on the Rue Popincourt. An overgrown child. He thought that he was studying man in the raw because he recorded scraps of conversations in cafés and in restaurants. These findings he labeled carefully, making a catalogue of them.

"I shall have to hear his recordings. Have you ever heard them?"

"He didn't let anyone hear them. Only once, I thought I heard a woman crying in his room. I went to see what was going on. He was alone, listening to one of his tapes. Have you any more questions to ask me?"

"Not just now. I shall probably come to your house sometime tomorrow, during the day. I suppose there are lots of people paying their respects."

"The doorbell never stops ringing. Oh well, that's that. I had hoped I would be of some use to you."

"Perhaps you have been, more than you think. Thank you for coming."

He took her to the door and shook hands with her. She was thrilled.

"Good-bye, Monsieur Maigret. Don't forget you promised I could hear the recordings with you."

He had not promised anything of the kind, but he decided not to argue.

What had he been doing when he had been given her card in his office? He had just come down from the magistrate's office.

"A scene right out of a film," he thought, grumbling.

And he remained in a more or less grumbling mood throughout the evening and a good part of the night. Because it wasn't just like a scene from any old film, but one from a real thriller, just the thing the men on the Rue des Saussaies were past masters at organizing.

At seven thirty, Lucas rang to say that the picture framer had closed the shutters and put up the wooden panel on the glass door. A little later he had gone to his usual restaurant for dinner. Then he walked around the block, as if he were just taking the air, then went to the Place de la Bastille, where he bought several magazines at a kiosk, then went home.

"What shall we do?"

"Wait."

As for Maigret and Janvier, they had dinner at the Brasserie Dauphine. It was almost empty. It was mainly at noon and before dinner that the two small rooms were crowded.

Maigret called up his wife just to say hello.

"I have no idea what time I'll be back. Certainly it will be very late. Unless it falls flat. I'm not in charge of the operation."

He was in charge of the men as long as they were in Paris and that was why, at nine o'clock, the car he was in, with Janvier at the wheel and fat Lourtie in the back, stopped in front of, or almost in front of, the picture framer's shop.

It was a black car with no distinctive marks, but fitted with a radio transmitter and receiver. Another car, exactly like it, equipped in the same way, was parked about fifty yards away. Superintendent Grosjean and three of his inspectors were sitting in it.

Finally, in a side street, there was a police van belonging to Criminal Investigation, with about ten plainclothes policemen inside.

Lucas was on watch, also in a car, not far from Mila's room on the Rue Notre-Dame-de-Lorette.

It was he who made the first move.

"Hello? 287? Is that you, Chief?"

"Maigret here."

"Lucas here. Mila has just left in a taxi. We are going through the center of the city and I think we are going to go over to the Left Bank."

At the same moment the door of the shop opened and the picture framer, who was wearing a lightweight beige overcoat, locked it behind him and walked briskly toward the Place de la Bastille.

"Hello, 215," Maigret called. "Is that you, Grosjean? Are you receiving me? Hello, 215?"

"215 here."

"We are about to move slowly toward the Place de la Bastille. He's on foot."

"Over?"

"Over."

Maigret shrugged his broad shoulders.

"Who ever would have thought I would be playing at cops and robbers!"

At the Place de la Bastille, Emile Branchu went toward the Boulevard Beaumarchais and opened the door of a black Citroën DS which moved off immediately.

Maigret could not see who was driving, probably the third man from the Café des Amis, the one who drank rum and had a scar on his face.

Grosjean followed at some distance. From time to time he called on the radio and a Maigret hating himself for being churlish replied. The van also stayed in radio contact.

The traffic was moving well. The DS was going fast and the driver did not appear to notice that he was being followed. Even less did he imagine that he was at the head of a little procession.

At the Porte de Châtillon he stopped for a moment and a tall, dark man standing at the edge of the sidewalk got into the car as if he did it every day of his life.

Now the three men were together. They too were organized in an almost military manner. They were going faster and Janvier had to adjust his speed so as not to lose them while still remaining unnoticed.

They had taken the road to Versailles and they went through Petit-Clamart hardly slackening their pace.

"Where are you?" Grosjean asked at regular intervals. "Are you keeping them in sight?"

"We're leaving my territory now," Maigret growled. "Now it's your turn."

"When we get wherever we're going."

They turned left toward Châtenay-Malabry, then right toward Jouy-en-Josas. There were thick clouds, some fairly low, but a good part of the sky was clear and the moon showed through.

The DS slowed, turned to the left again, and soon could be heard braking.

"Shall I stop here?" asked Janvier. "I think they have stopped. . . . Yes, they have stopped."

Lourtie got out to see. When he came back he announced:

"They've met someone who was waiting for them. They went into a big garden or park, I don't know which. I could see the roof of a villa."

Grosjean, lost in the country lanes, asked what was going on, and Maigret brought him up to date.

"Where did you say you are?"

And Lourtie whispered:

"Chemin des Acacias. I saw the sign."

"Chemin des Acacias."

Lourtie went to take up his post at the corner of the road where Mila and his companions had got out of the car. They had left the DS at the edge of the road. The lookout was still there, but the other three seemed to have gone into the house.

The Criminal Investigation car finally parked behind Maigret's, then, a few moments later, the impressive van stuffed with policemen joined them.

"Over to you now," Maigret breathed, filling his pipe.

"Where are they?"

"Almost certainly in the villa whose gate you can see from the corner. The man on the sidewalk is their lookout."

"Will you come with me?"

"I'll stay here."

Some moments later, Grosjean's car swung into the road on the left so suddenly that the lookout, caught by surprise, had no time to give the alarm. Before he knew what had happened to him, two men had grabbed him and handcuffed him.

Policemen hurtled out of the van into the grounds of the villa, which they surrounded hastily, cutting off all exits. It was a modern building, fairly large, and the water that could be seen glinting through the trees was that of the swimming pool.

All the windows were dark, the shutters closed. Nevertheless, footsteps could be heard, and when the men of Criminal Investigation, with Grosjean at their head, opened the door, they found themselves facing three men in rubber gloves who, having heard strange noises, were trying to get out.

They made no attempt to escape, raised their hands

above their heads, and a few seconds later they too were handcuffed.

"Put them in the van. I'll question them when we get back to my office."

Maigret was walking up and down stretching his legs. From a distance he watched the men being pushed into the van, then he saw Grosjean coming toward him.

"Aren't you coming with me to have a look at the inside?"

The first thing they noticed was a marble plaque to the right of the gate which said, in gilded letters, "The Golden Crown." A crown, carved in the stone, made Maigret think of something. What was it? He couldn't remember.

There was no corridor. One entered, on the same level, an immense room where hunting trophies and paintings alternated on the white stone walls. One of the pictures had been taken down and was lying upside down on a mahogany table.

"A Cézanne," murmured Grosjean, who had turned it over.

In a corner there was a Louis XV desk. The leather blotting pad bore the same crown as the plaque at the gate. In a drawer there were writing paper and envelopes with the same crown and below that the name Philippe Lherbier.

"Look at this, Grosjean."

He showed him the crown on the blotting pad, then the writing paper.

"Do you get it? The famous leather merchant on the Rue Royale."

He was a man of sixty with a thick head of snow-white hair that made his face look fresher and younger.

Not only was his shop the most elegant place in which

71

to buy leather in Paris, but he owned branches in Cannes, Deauville, London, New York, and Miami.

"What shall I do? Telephone him?"

"That's up to you, my friend."

Grosjean lifted the receiver and dialed the number on the writing paper.

"Hello. . . . Is this Monsieur Lherbier's residence? . . . Yes, Monsieur Philippe Lherbier. . . . He's not at home? . . . Have you any idea where I might reach him? . . . What's that? . . . At the home of Maître Legendre, Boulevard Saint-Germain. . . . Can you tell me the number?"

He took a pencil from his pocket and scribbled some figures on the beautiful crown-embossed paper.

Legendre the lawyer also belonged to the upper ranks of Parisian society.

Maigret looked at the paintings. Two more Cézannes, a Derain, a Sisley. He pushed open a door and found a smaller, more feminine drawing room, its walls hung with buttercup-yellow silk. It reminded him of the house on the Quai d'Anjou. He had landed back in the same world, and undoubtedly the two men knew each other, if only through meeting in the places they both frequented.

Philippe Lherbier was often the subject of newspaper gossip, particularly for his marriages and divorces. He was called the most-divorced man in France. Was it five times? Six?

The strangest thing was that after each divorce he married again in less than six months. Always to the same kind of woman! All of them, except one who was an actress, had been tall, slim models with more or less fixed smiles. One would have thought that he married them only to be able to dress them sumptuously and to have them play a purely decorative role.

"Yes. . . . Thank you for getting him. . . . Hello? . . .

72

Is that Monsieur Lherbier? . . . Superintendent Grosjean of Criminal Investigation here. . . . I'm in your villa at Jouy-en-Josas. . . . What am I doing here? . . . I have just arrested three burglars who were making off with your pictures. . . ."

Grosjean put his hand over the mouthpiece and whispered to Maigret: "He's laughing. . . ."

Then, in a normal voice:

"What's that? . . . Yours are insured? That's good. . . . You're not coming out this evening? . . . Well, I can't leave the place open and I have no way of locking it up. That means that one of my men will have to stay in the villa until you send someone with, among other things, a locksmith. . . . I must . . ."

He stood still a moment, listening, his face very red.

"He hung up," he murmured finally.

He was furious at having been cut off while he was speaking.

"That's the kind of person for whom we . . . we . . ."

He undoubtedly would have added:

"For whom we risk our lives."

But he realized that in the present situation that seemed to be rather overstating the case.

"I don't know if he was drunk, but he sounded as if he thought the whole thing was a huge joke."

He detailed one of his men to remain in the villa until further notice.

"Are you coming, Maigret?"

Maigret was not yet ready to leave.

"Cézannes . . . And . . . it doesn't matter. Hundreds of thousands of francs' worth of pictures in a villa he only uses on weekends.

"He has an even bigger villa at Cap d'Antibes. It's called 'The Golden Crown' too. If the papers are to be be-

73

lieved, he has his cigars and cigarettes marked with the same gold crown. His yacht is called 'The Golden Crown.' . . ."

"Really?" breathed Grosjean, incredulous.

"It seems to be true."

"Doesn't anyone laugh at him?"

"They're all vying for invitations to one of his houses."

They found themselves outside again and stopped for a moment to look at the swimming pool, which must have been heated, for a thin cloud of vapor rose from it.

"Are you coming to the Rue des Saussaies?"

"No. The robbery is none of my business, because it didn't take place within my jurisdiction. The only thing I would like, tomorrow if possible, is to question them on another matter. Poiret would like to hear what they have to say, too."

"The Rue Popincourt case?"

"That's how we got on their tracks."

"That's true. I'd forgotten."

When they were back at the cars, the two men shook hands, each one about as stout as the other, each with the same career behind him, the same experiences.

"I'll be there for the rest of the night. Oh, well . . ."

Maigret got in beside Janvier. Lourtie, sitting behind, was smoking a cigarette which made a small red glow in the dark.

"Well, that's that. Up to now we've only been working for the Criminal Investigation boys. Tomorrow we'll try to do our own work."

And Janvier, alluding to the lack of cordiality that had always existed between the two branches of the police, asked:

"Do you think they'll let us see them?"

Chapter **4**   It must have been a busy night on the Rue des Saussaies, where the reporters and photographers, alerted as usual God only knows how, were quick to arrive and invade the corridors.

At half past seven Maigret switched on the radio automatically, while he was shaving. It was time for the news and, as if it were what he had been expecting, they were talking about the villa in Jouy-en-Josas and the well-known millionaire Philippe Lherbier, the man of the six wives and the golden crowns.

"Four men are under lock and key, but Superintendent Grosjean remains convinced that none of them is the real head of the gang, the mastermind. Besides, rumor has it that Superintendent Maigret may intervene, not in the picture-stealing case, but about some other matter the criminals may be involved in. This is being kept a great secret. . . ."

He learned another piece of news from the radio: the three robbers and the lookout had not been armed.

He was in his office at nine o'clock, and immediately after the briefing he telephoned Grosjean at the Rue des Saussaies.

"Did you get any sleep?"

"Less than three hours. I had to be a bit rough with them. None of them will say anything. One of them, in particular, makes me see red. It's Julien Mila, the bartender, the most intelligent of the three. Whenever you ask him any questions, he gives you a mocking look and says in a soft voice:

75

" 'Unfortunately, I have nothing to say.' "

"Haven't they asked to see their lawyers?"

"Of course they have. Maître Huet, naturally. He's coming to see me this morning."

"When can you send them over to me? Poiret, the magistrate, wants to see them too."

"Sometime this afternoon, I hope. I expect you'll have to give them back to me, because I imagine I'll need a long time with them yet. The list of burglaries of the same type that have been committed around Paris in the last two years is a long one—at least twelve—and I'm sure that they are responsible for most of them, if not all. And you? What about the Rue Popincourt case?"

"Nothing new."

"Do you think these characters I've got have anything to do with it?"

"I don't know. One of the thieves, the small, broad-shouldered one with a scar on his face, was wearing a light-colored, belted raincoat, wasn't he? And a brown hat?"

"Demarle. Yes, he was. We're looking at his record. He seems to be a tough one, and he's come up against the law more than once."

"What about Branchu, the one they call Mimile? The picture framer?"

"No criminal record. He lived for a long time in Marseilles but he comes from Roubaix."

"See you before long."

The newspapers published photographs of the handcuffed criminals on the front page, together with a photograph of the leather merchant at the weigh-in at Longchamp, in tails with a pale gray topper.

Mila was looking at the camera with an ironic smile. Demarle, the scarred sailor, looked completely surprised at what was happening to him, while the picture framer held his hands over his face. As for the lookout, badly dressed in a suit too big for him, he looked like a nonentity of rather limited intelligence.

"After an investigation which Divisional Superintendent Grosjean of Criminal Investigation has been carrying out for nearly two years, a good haul . . ."

Maigret shrugged his shoulders. It wasn't so much the thieves he was thinking about as, in spite of himself, Antoine Batille. He had often said that it was almost always by getting to know the victim that one was led to the murderer.

There was a thin sun. The sky was a very pale blue. The temperature remained at 2 or 3 degrees Centigrade, and it was freezing in most of France, except on the west coast.

He put on his coat, picked up his hat, and went through the inspectors' office.

"I'm going out for about an hour."

Alone, for once. He wanted to go alone to the Quai d'Anjou. He walked there along the *quais* as far as the Pont-Marie, which he crossed. He smoked his pipe slowly and kept his hands stuffed in his pockets.

In his mind he was going over the ground the young man with the tape recorder had covered that night, the night of March 18th–19th, which was to be his last night.

Already, from a good distance away, he could see the black hangings surrounding the doorway with, in silver, an enormous "B," fringes, and teardrops. As he passed by the lodge he saw the concierge, who was watching the comings and goings.

She was still young, attractive. Her black dress was

brightened up by a white collar and cuffs that gave it the look of a uniform. He wondered whether to go into the lodge, not because he had reason to, but because he was casting about in all directions.

He did not go in but took the elevator. The door of the Batilles' apartment was shut. He pushed it open and went toward the little drawing room which had been turned into a mortuary chapel. A very dignified old woman was standing by the door and nodded to him. Was she a relative? A friend or a nanny who was representing the family?

A man was standing holding his hat in front of him, moving his lips in prayer. A woman, probably a local shopkeeper, was kneeling at a *prie-dieu*.

Antoine had not yet been put into his coffin but was laid out on the couch, his clasped hands entwined with a rosary.

In the flickering light of the candles his face looked very young. He could have been fifteen years old as easily as twenty. Not only had he been shaved, but his hair had been cut, undoubtedly so that those who came to pay their respects should not take him for a hippie.

Maigret too moved his lips, mechanically, without conviction, then went back into the entrance hall, looking for someone he might speak to. He found a manservant in a striped waistcoat who was vacuum-cleaning the large drawing room.

"I should like to see Mademoiselle Batille," he said. "I am Superintendent Maigret."

The servant hesitated and finally went off, grumbling: "If she's up."

She was, but she obviously wasn't ready, because he had to wait at least ten minutes and when she appeared she was wearing her peignoir, her bare feet stuck into a pair of mules.

"Have you found out something?"

"No. I only wanted to see your brother's room."

"Do forgive me for receiving you like this, but I slept very badly and anyway I'm not used to getting up early."

"Is your father in?"

"No. He had to go to the office. Mother's in her room, but I haven't seen her yet this morning."

They went along the hall, then along another that cut across the first at right angles. As they passed an open door through which Maigret saw an unmade bed and a breakfast tray, she explained: "That's my room. Don't look at it. It's very untidy."

Antoine's room was two doors farther along. It looked out onto the courtyard and at that time of day gathered in the sun's oblique rays. The Scandinavian furniture was simple and harmonious. On a stretch of wall there were shelves full of books, records, and, on two shelves, cassette tapes.

On the desk there were books, notebooks, colored pencils, and, in a glass dish, three miniature tortoises swimming in about three quarters of an inch of water.

"Was your brother fond of animals?"

"He had grown out of it a bit. There was a time when he brought home all kinds of creatures, a crow with a broken wing, for example, hamsters, white mice, a snake more than a yard long. He tried to tame them but he never succeeded."

There was also an enormous globe on a stand, and a flute lying on a table, and some sheet music.

"Did he play the flute?"

"He had five or six lessons. There must be an electric guitar around somewhere too. He took piano lessons. . . ."

Maigret smiled.

"Not for long, I imagine."

"His enthusiasms never lasted long."

"Except for his tape recorder."

"That's true. That craze has lasted for nearly a year."

"Did he have any idea what he was going to do with his future?"

"No. Or if he did he didn't tell anyone. Papa would have liked him to enroll in the Faculty of Science and take a degree in Chemistry, so that he could take over the business later."

"He didn't agree?"

"He hated the business world. I think he was ashamed to be the son of Mylène perfumes."

"How do you feel about it?"

"I don't care one way or the other."

One felt at ease in that room, among objects of an incongruous variety, it is true, but one had the feeling that they were well-loved things. Someone had really lived in that room and had made it his kingdom.

At random, Maigret picked out one of the cassettes on the shelves, but there was only a number on it.

"The notebook he used as a catalogue should be here," said Minou. "Wait a minute."

She opened and shut drawers, most of them full. Certain objects and papers must have dated from his first years at the lycée.

"Here. I should think it's up-to-date, because he took it very seriously."

It was an ordinary notebook with square-ruled paper. On the cover, Antoine had written "My Experiences" in ornate lettering, with pencils of various colors.

It began with:

"Cassette 1: The family at table one Sunday."

"Why a Sunday?" Maigret asked.

"Because my father rarely comes home to lunch on weekdays. And in the evening my mother and he often have dinner in town, or they have guests. . . ."

So he had reserved his first recording for the family.

"Cassett 2: The southern highway one Saturday evening."

"Cassette 3: Forest of Fontainebleau, at night."

"Cassette 4: The métro at 8 p.m."

"Cassette 5: Noon on the Place de l'Opéra."

Then there was an intermission at the Théâtre de la Gymnase, the sounds of a supermarket on the Rue de Ponthieu, and the drugstore on the Champs-Elysées.

"Cassette 10: A café in Puteaux."

His curiosity began to cover a wider field and by slow degrees he changed social strata: a factory at closing time, dance halls on the Rue de Lappe, a bar on the Rue des Gravilliers, the neighborhood of the Saint-Martin canal, the Bal des Fleurs at La Villette, a café at Saint-Denis.

He was no longer interested in the center of Paris but in the periphery, and one of the addresses was on the edge of a shanty-town built out of tin cans and boxes.

"Was it really dangerous?"

"More or less. Let's say it wasn't to be recommended, and he was right not to take you with him. The people who frequent such places don't like anyone sticking his nose into their affairs, particularly with a tape recorder."

"Do you think that's why . . . ?"

"I don't know. I'm doubtful. To be sure, I'd have to hear all his tapes. From what I can see, that would take hours, if not several days."

"You're not going to do that?"

"If I could take them away for a while I would give one of my detectives the job of . . ."

"I couldn't dare take that responsibility on my own. Since his death, my brother has become sacred and everything that was his has taken on a new value. Do you understand? Before, they treated him rather like an overgrown schoolboy, which made him furious. It's true that in certain respects he had remained very young. . . ."

Maigret's glance slid over the walls, over nude photographs cut out of an American magazine.

"That's very young too," she interrupted his thoughts. "I'm sure my brother never slept with a girl. He went out with two or three of my friends but never went all the way. . . ."

"Did he have a car?"

"My parents gave him a little English car for his twentieth birthday. For two months he spent all his time out in the country and he fitted the car out with every imaginable accessory. After that he wasn't interested in it any more and he only took it out when he really needed it."

"Not for his nocturnal expeditions?"

"Never. I'm going to ask Mother if I can let you have the cassettes. I hope she's up."

It was ten thirty. The girl was away for quite some time.

"She trusts you," she announced on her return. "All she wants is for you to catch the murderer. By the way, my father is even more overwhelmed than she is. It was his only son. Since it happened, he doesn't speak to us and he goes off early to the office. . . . How are we going to wrap that up? It needs a suitcase, or a big box. A suitcase would be best. Hold on—I think I know where to find what we need."

The suitcase she brought in a few moments later bore

the golden crown of the leather merchant of the Rue Royale.

"Do you know Philippe Lherbier?"

"My parents know him. They've been to dinner at his house two or three times, but he's not what you might call a friend. He's the man who's always getting divorced, isn't he?"

"His country house was burgled last night. Didn't you hear the radio?"

"I only listen to it on the beach, for the music."

She helped him to stack the cassettes in the suitcase, and she added the notebook that served as a catalogue.

"Haven't you anything more to ask me? You can come and question me at any time and I promise you I'll answer as frankly as I have up till now."

She was clearly excited to be helping the police.

"I won't show you out, because I'm not dressed for going past the room where he is. People would take that as a lack of respect. Why must they suddenly respect someone when he's dead, when they didn't pay any attention to him when he was alive?"

Maigret went out, a little embarrassed by his suitcase, especially when he passed the concierge. He was lucky enough to see a woman get out of a taxi and pay the driver, so that he didn't have to wait to find one.

"Quai des Orfèvres."

He wondered whom he would give Antoine Batille's tape recordings to. It had to be someone who knew the places where the recordings had been made and who was familiar with the people who frequented them.

He ended up by going to the end of the corridor to find his colleague in the Social Division—a euphemism for the Vice Squad.

Since he was carrying the suitcase, his colleague asked ironically:

"Have you come to say good-bye before leaving us for good?"

"I have some tape recordings here, most of them made around the periphery of Paris—dance halls, cafés, bistrots. . . ."

"Should I be interested?"

"Perhaps not, but I am, and they may have a connection with a case I have in hand."

"The Rue Popincourt case?"

"Just between you and me, yes. I would rather no one else knew that. You must have someone among your men who knows those places and to whom these recordings might mean something."

"I understand. Nose out a dangerous character, for example. A man who, if he was afraid he'd be incriminated . . ."

"That's it exactly."

"Old Mangeot. He has almost forty years' service. He knows the fauna of those places better than anyone."

Maigret knew him.

"Is he free?"

"I'll fix it so that he is."

"Does he know how to work those things? I'll go and get the tape recorder from my office."

When he came back a sad-faced man, soft-featured, no sparkle in his eyes, was standing in the office of the Vice Squad chief.

He was one of the little men of the Criminal Police, one of those who, through the lack of a certain basic education, remain unpromoted all their lives. These men, since they go all over Paris on foot, acquire the walk of maîtres d'hôtel and waiters, people who are on their feet all day. One might even say that they become the same dull color as the poor streets they pace along.

"I know how to work those things," he said at once. "Are there a lot of cassettes?"

"About fifty—maybe a few more."

"At half an hour per cassette . . . Is it urgent?"

"Quite."

"I'll give him an office where he won't be disturbed," intervened the chief of the erstwhile Vice Squad.

They explained carefully to Mangeot what was expected of him, and he nodded to show that he understood, then went off carrying the suitcase while Maigret's colleague murmured:

"Don't worry. He looks senile. It's true that he has no illusions left, but he's still one of my best men. A sort of bloodhound. You let him get the scent and he's off, head down. . . ."

Maigret went back to his office, and ten minutes later the magistrate telephoned him.

"I've tried several times to get you since . . . First of all, I must congratulate you on last night's haul."

"The men from the Rue des Saussaies did it all."

"I've been to see the public prosecutor, who is delighted. They're bringing me the four scoundrels at three this afternoon. I'd like you to be in my office, because you know the case better than I do. When I've finished with the burglaries you can take them down to your office if you think fit. I know you have your own way of carrying out your interrogations."

"Thank you. I'll be in your office at three o'clock."

He pushed open the door of the inspectors' office.

"Are you free for lunch, Janvier?"

"Yes, Chief. I just have to finish my report and then . . ."

Always reports and paperwork.

"What about you, Lapointe?"

"You know I'm always free. . . ."

For that meant that the three of them were going to have lunch together in the Brasserie Dauphine.

"Meet you at twelve thirty."

Maigret remembered to telephone his wife and she, as usual, did not fail to ask:

"Do you think you'll be back for dinner? It's a pity about lunch. I'd got snails."

As if by chance, each time that he did not go home for a meal, the dish that had been prepared was one that he particularly liked.

After all, there might be snails at the Brasserie Dauphine, too.

When, at three o'clock, Maigret entered the long corridor with magistrates' offices opening off it on both sides, photographers' flashguns went off while ten or eleven reporters rushed toward him.

"Have you come to listen to the interrogation of the gang?"

He tried to slip through without answering yes or no.

"Why are you here, and not Superintendent Grosjean?"

"For heaven's sake, I don't know. Ask the magistrate."

"You're in charge of the Rue Popincourt case, aren't you?"

He had no reason to deny it.

"Might there be a connection between the two cases?"

"Gentlemen, I have nothing to say at the moment."

"But you aren't denying it?"

"You'd be making a mistake to draw any conclusions."

"You were at Jouy-en-Josas last night, weren't you?"

"I don't deny that."

"Why?"

"My colleague Grosjean can tell you that better than I."

"Did your men get on the track of the thieves in Paris?"

The four men arrested the previous night were seated on two benches, one on each side of the magistrate's door, handcuffed and between policemen, and they were watching the scene not without some amusement.

At the far end of the corridor a counsel appeared, a short man, but broad. He was robed and looked as if he were flapping his wings. When he saw the superintendent he walked over to him and shook him by the hand.

"How are you, Maigret?"

A flash. The handshake had been photographed just as if the scene had been rehearsed.

"Why are you here, anyway?"

Maître Huet asked this question in front of the photographers, and he did not do so by chance. He was a clever man, wily even, who was accustomed to defending the big gangsters. A very cultivated man, a lover of music and the theater, he was at all the first nights and went to all the big concerts, which had made him a part of fashionable Paris.

"Why are we waiting to go in?"

"I don't know," replied Maigret, not without irony.

And the small, broad-shouldered man knocked at the magistrate's door, pushed it open, and motioned the superintendent to go in with him.

"How do you do, my dear Magistrate. I hope you aren't too upset at seeing me here. My clients . . ."

The magistrate shook hands with him and then with Maigret.

"Sit down, gentlemen. I'm going to have the prisoners brought in. I assume they won't frighten you and that I can leave the policemen outside?"

He had the handcuffs removed. The office, which was not large, was full. The clerk sat at one end of the table which served as a desk. They had to look for an extra chair in a storeroom. The four men sat on both sides of their lawyer and Maigret sat a little apart, in the background.

"As you know, Maître, I must first establish the identity of the prisoners. Each of you answer when I call out your name. Julien Mila."

"Here."

"Your surname, Christian names, place of residence, date and place of birth, profession. . . ."

"Mila with a 't'?" asked the clerk who was writing it all down.

"Just with an 'a'."

That took a long time. Demarle, the man with the scar and the muscles of a fairground wrestler, had been born in Quimper. He had been a sailor and was at present on relief.

"Your address?"

"Sometimes here, sometimes there. I can always find a friend who'll take me in."

"So in other words you have no fixed address?"

"Well, with what we get on relief . . ."

The lookout was a poor, unhealthy-looking man who said that he was a messenger and that he lived on the Rue du Mont-Cenis, in Montmartre.

"How long have you been a member of the gang?"

"Excuse me, Magistrate," Huet interrupted. "It must first be established that there is a gang, and . . ."

"I was just about to ask you a question, Maître. Which of these men do you represent?"

"All four of them."

"Do you not think that in the course of the interrogation there might be a conflict between them due to a divergence of interests?"

"I very much doubt it, and if it should happen I would have recourse to a colleague. Does that suit you, gentlemen?"

All four nodded.

"Since we are dealing with preliminary questions, I might say with questions of ethics," Huet continued with a smile that boded ill, "you should know that since this morning there has been a great deal of interest shown in the case by the press. I have had a great number of telephone calls and through them I have obtained information that has surprised, not to say shocked, me."

He turned his back and lit a cigarette. The magistrate, confronted by such a shining light of the legal profession, could not but be nervous.

"Go on."

"The arrest, in fact, was not made in the way that is usual in arrests of this nature. Three radio cars, one of them filled with plain-clothes detectives, arrived on the scene at approximately the same time as my clients, as if the police knew what was going to happen. And, at the head of this procession, we find Superintendent Maigret, whom we have here with us, and two of his colleagues. Is that not so, Superintendent?"

"That is so."

"I see that my informant was not mistaken."

Someone from the Rue des Saussaies probably, perhaps a clerk or a typist.

"I believed, I have always believed, that the territory covered by the Criminal Police was limited to Paris. Let us say, to Greater Paris, and Jouy-en-Josas does not even belong to that."

He had got what he wanted. He had forced the direction of the questioning and the magistrate did not know how to silence him.

"Would it not be because the information about this, let us say this attempted burglary, came to the ears of the Criminal Police? Have you nothing to say, Maigret?"

"I have nothing to say."

"Were you not there?"

"I am not here to be questioned."

"Nevertheless, I am going to ask you another, more important question. Is it not true that while you were dealing with another case, itself a recent one, you chanced on this one?"

Maigret still did not reply.

"Maître, please," interrupted the magistrate.

"One moment. Detectives of the Criminal Police were pointed out to me as having kept watch these past two days opposite Emile Branchu's shop. Superintendent Maigret himself was seen twice day before yesterday in a café on the Place de la Bastille where my clients meet from time to time, and he questioned the waiters and tried to extract information from the proprietor. Is that not so? Forgive me, Magistrate, but I have to put this case in its true perspective, which is perhaps not that of which you are aware."

"Have you finished, Maître?"

"For the time being."

"May I question the first prisoner? Julien Mila, be so good as to tell me who pointed out Philippe Lherbier's villa to you and who told you about the valuable paintings in it."

"I advise my client not to answer."

"I shall not answer."

"You are suspected of having taken part in twenty-one

burglaries of villas and châteaux that have occurred under the same conditions in the past two years."

"I have nothing to say."

"Particularly," interrupted the lawyer, "since you have no proof."

"I shall repeat my first question, making it more general. Who pointed out these villas and châteaux to you? Who—and it is obviously the same person—took the responsibility of selling the stolen paintings and *objets d'art*?"

"I don't know a thing about any of that."

The magistrate, sighing, moved on to the picture framer, and Mimile was no more talkative. As for Demarle-the-Sailor, he amused himself by being funny.

The only one to have a different attitude was the lookout, the man called Gouvion.

"I don't know why I'm here. I don't know these men. I was around there looking for a place to sleep that wouldn't be too cold."

"Is that your point of view, Maître?"

"I am in complete agreement with what he says and I must point out to you that this man has no criminal record."

"Has no one anything to add?"

"I want to ask one question, at the risk of repeating myself. What part does Superintendent Maigret play in this? And what is going to happen once we leave this office?"

"I do not have to answer you."

"Does that mean that there is going to be another interrogation, not in the Law Courts, but in one of the offices of the Criminal Police, where I have no right of entry? In other words, will it be a question not of a burglary but of quite another case?"

"I am sorry, Maître, but I have nothing to say to you. Please ask your clients to sign the provisional report which will be typed, in quadruplicate, by tomorrow."

"You may sign, gentlemen."

"Thank you, Maître."

And, getting up, the magistrate went toward the door, followed closely by the lawyer.

"I have made all my objections."

"And I have noted them."

Then, to the policemen:

"Put the handcuffs back on the prisoners and take them to the Criminal Police. You may go through the communicating door. Would you wait here a moment, please, Superintendent?"

Maigret sat down again.

"What do you think?"

"I think that at this very moment Maître Huet is busy telling the press all about it and making it seem absurdly important, so that by tomorrow, even by tonight in the later editions, it will run to two columns."

"Does that worry you?"

"I'm not sure. A few moments ago I would have said yes. My intention was to keep the two cases quite separate from each other and to keep the papers from mixing them up. But now . . ."

He reflected, weighed the pros and cons.

"Perhaps it's better this way. If they stir things up, there's a chance that . . ."

"Do you think that one of those four men . . ."

"I can't say anything for sure. It seems that a Swedish knife like the one used on the Rue Popincourt has been found in the sailor's pocket. The man was wearing a light-colored, belted raincoat and a brown hat. In any case, probably this evening, I shall let the Pagliatis see him, in the same street, under the same lighting conditions, but that wouldn't be conclusive. The old woman from the first floor will be called to identify him too."

"What are you hoping for?"

"I don't know. The burglaries are the affair of the Rue des Saussaies. What I'm interested in are the seven stab wounds that took a young man's life."

When he left the magistrate's office, the reporters had disappeared, but he found them in full strength—more of them, even—in the corridor of the Criminal Police. The four suspects were not in sight, for they had been taken into an office where they would be out of the public eye.

"What's going on, Superintendent?"

"Nothing out of the ordinary."

"Why are those four men here instead of being taken back to the Rue des Saussaies?"

"Well, I'll tell you. . . ."

He made a sudden decision. Huet had certainly told them that there was a connection between the two cases. Instead of seeing them publish information that was true and false in varying degrees, would it not be better to tell them the truth?

"Antoine Batille, gentlemen, had one passion in life: to record what he called 'living documents.' With his tape recorder slung over his shoulder, he went into public places, cafés, bars, dance halls, restaurants, even into the métro, and quietly switched on his toy.

"On Tuesday evening, at about nine thirty, he was in a café on the Place de la Bastille and, as usual, he had turned his instrument on. His neighbors were . . ."

"The thieves?"

"Three of them. The lookout was not there. The recording is not very good. Still, one can hear that a meeting had been arranged for the day after next, and that a certain villa was even then being given the once-over.

"Less than an hour later, on the Rue Popincourt, the young man was attacked from behind and stabbed seven times, one of the wounds being fatal."

"Do you think it was one of these men?"

"I don't think anything, gentlemen. My job is not to think, but to get proofs or confessions."

"Did anyone see the assailant?"

"Two passers-by, some distance away, and a lady living right opposite the spot where the murder was committed."

"Do you think that the thieves realized that their plans had been recorded?"

"Again, I don't think anything. It's a plausible hypothesis."

"In that case Batille must have been followed by one of them until he was in a quiet enough spot and . . . Did the murderer take the tape recorder away?"

"No."

"How do you explain that?"

"I don't explain it."

"The passers-by you mentioned. I suppose you mean the Pagliati couple. You see, we know more than one might suppose. When they started to run, then, did the Pagliatis stop the man from . . ."

"No. He had only struck four times. After going off, he came back on his tracks to strike again three more times. So he could have snatched the tape recorder from the victim's neck."

"So you're really nowhere?"

"I am going to question these gentlemen."

"Together?"

"One by one."

"Beginning with which one?"

"With Yvon Demarle, the sailor."

"When will you have finished?"

"I don't know. One of you can stay here. . . ."

"And the rest of us go and have a beer! That's a good idea! Thanks, Superintendent."

Maigret too would gladly have had a beer. He went into his office and called in Lapointe, who could take shorthand.

"Sit there. Take it all down."

Then, to Janvier:

"Go and get me Demarle, will you?"

The ex-sailor appeared, his hands together in front of him.

"Take the handcuffs off. Sit down, Demarle."

"What are you going to do to me? Grill me? I might as well tell you right now that I'm tough and I won't let myself be trapped."

"Is that all?"

"I just wonder why I could have a lawyer with me up there, and here I'm all by myself."

"Maître Huet will tell you about that when he sees you again. There was a Swedish knife among the objects taken from you. . . ."

"Is that why you've brought me here? I've carried that in my pocket for twenty years. It was a present from my brother, when I was still a fisherman in Quimper, before I went on the liners."

"How long is it since you've used it?"

"I use it every day to cut up my meat, country style. Maybe it's not very elegant, but . . ."

"On Tuesday evening you were in the Café des Amis, on the Place de la Bastille, with your two friends."

"That's what you say. But I can never remember in the morning what I did the night before. I don't seem to have a very good head."

"Mila was there, and the picture framer, and you. You talked, in more or less guarded words, about the burglary, and you were given the job, among other things, of getting a car. Where did you steal it from?"

"What?"

"The car."

"What car?"

"I suppose you don't know where the Rue Popincourt is, either?"

"I don't come from Paris."

"Did none of the three of you notice that a young man at the next table had switched on a tape recorder?"

"A what?"

"You didn't follow that young man?"

"Why should I? Believe me, I'm not that kind."

"Your confederates didn't order you to come back with the cassette?"

"That's great! A cassette, now. Is that all?"

"That's all."

And, to Janvier:

"Take him to an empty office. The same thing."

Janvier was to repeat the questions, more or less in the same words and in the same order. When he had finished, another inspector would take over.

Maigret didn't pin his hopes on it, in the circumstances, but it was still the most effective method. It could go on for hours. One interrogation like that had gone on for thirty-six hours before the man concerned, who had come in as a witness, confessed his crime. Three or four times during the interrogation the policemen had been on the point of releasing him, so well did he play the innocent.

Maigret went in to the inspectors' office. "Go and get Mila for me," he said to Lourtie.

The bartender knew very well he was a good-looking man, more intelligent, more aware than the others. One would swear that he enjoyed the part he was playing.

"Oh! Isn't my mouthpiece here?"

He pretended to look around for the lawyer.

"Do you think it's in order for you to question me when he isn't here?"

"That's my business."

"What I mean is, I wouldn't like the whole procedure to be declared irregular because of one little thing."

"What was the reason for your first conviction?"

"I don't remember. Anyway, it's up there, in Records. You see, even if I haven't had anything to do with you personally, I know the place a bit."

"When did you realize that your conversation was being recorded?"

"What conversation are you talking about, and what recording?"

Maigret was patient enough to ask his questions to the very end, although he knew all the time that there was no point. And Lourtie would repeat them untiringly, just as Janvier was now doing with the sailor.

Then it was the picture framer's turn. At first he seemed timid, but he was just as unshakable as the others.

"How long have you been burgling unoccupied houses?"

"I beg your pardon?"

"I said how long . . ."

Maigret was hot and the sweat stuck to his back. The men had arranged things among themselves. Each one played his part without letting himself be taken unawares by any unexpected question.

97

The messenger-tramp held to his story. First, he wasn't at the meeting on the Place de la Bastille. Then, on that Thursday evening, he was looking for a "pad," as he called it.

"In an empty house?"

"As long as the door is open . . . In the house or in the garage."

At six o'clock in the evening the four men went back in a police car to the Rue des Saussaies, where they spent the night.

"Is that you, Grosjean? Thank you for lending them to me. No, I didn't get anything out of them. They're no choirboys."

"Who do you think you're telling! Thursday's burglary, that'll stick, since they were caught in the act. But as for the other burglaries, if we don't get any proof or any witnesses . . ."

"You'll see, when the papers come out with it, witnesses will spring up all over."

"Do you still think one of those four did the job on the Rue Popincourt?"

"Not really."

"Have you any ideas about it?"

"No."

"What are you going to do?"

"Wait."

And that was true. Already the evening papers were publishing in their final editions the account of what had happened in the corridor outside the magistrate's office and then the statement Maigret had made in the Criminal Police.

Is this the Rue Popincourt murderer?

Below this question was the photograph of Yvon Demarle, handcuffed, by Magistrate Poiret's door.

Maigret looked in the telephone directory for the number of the apartment on the Quai d'Anjou, and dialed it.

"Hello, who is speaking?"

"This is Monsieur Batille's valet."

"Is Monsieur Batille at home just now?"

"He has not come home yet. I think he has an appointment to see his doctor."

"This is Superintendent Maigret. When is the funeral?"

"Tomorrow at ten."

"Thank you."

At last! Maigret's day was over and he called his wife to say he'd be back for dinner.

"We'll go to the movies afterward," he added.

To get things out of his mind.

Chapter **5**   Just to make sure, Maigret had young Lapointe go with him. They both stood in the crowd, on the embankment side of the street, not opposite the house of the dead boy but opposite the house next door, for there were so many onlookers that they had not been able to get a better place.

There were cars, among them many chauffeur-driven limousines, all along the embankments from the Pont Louis-Philippe to the Pont-Sully, and others were parked on the other side of the island on the Quai de Béthune and the Quai d'Orléans.

It was a cold morning, the weather what is called crisp, very clear, very bright, pastel-colored.

They saw the cars stop in front of the black-draped front door, people go upstairs, where they bowed toward the coffin before reappearing and waiting outside for the procession to form.

A red-haired photographer, bareheaded, walked about pointing his lens at the rows of spectators. He was not always well received, and some of them did not hesitate to tell him what they thought of him.

He still went on with his work, unmoved. The people, especially those who grumbled, would have been very surprised to learn that he did not belong to a newspaper, a photo agency, or a magazine, but that he was there on Maigret's orders.

Maigret had gone up to the Criminal Identity laboratory very early and, with Moers's help, had chosen

100

Van Hamme, the best and, more important, the most resourceful of the available photographers.

"I want photographs of all the onlookers, first outside the house, then outside the church, when the coffin is taken in and again when it comes out, and finally at the cemetery.

"When the pictures are developed, look at them carefully with a magnifying glass. It's possible that one or more people will be at all three places. Those are the ones I'm interested in. You'll need to enlarge them for me, without the surrounding figures."

In spite of himself, Maigret was looking for a light-colored, belted raincoat and a dark hat. There was not much chance that the murderer had kept those clothes, for the morning papers had described them. For the present the two cases, the Rue Popincourt case and the burglary, were definitively intertwined.

In one of the papers, under the picture of Demarle-the-Sailor, in his raincoat and brown hat, was printed:

IS THIS THE MURDERER?

The crowd was a mixture of types. First of all, near the house, were those who had been to pay their last respects to the dead boy and who were waiting to take their place in the procession. On the edge of the sidewalk it was mostly those who lived on the island, the concierges and the shopkeepers of the Rue Saint-Louis-en-l'Ile.

"Such a nice boy! . . . And so shy! . . . When he came into the shop he always tipped his hat. . . ."

"If only he had had his hair cut a little shorter. . . . His parents should have told him. . . . Elegant people like them! . . . It made him look like the wrong kind. . . ."

From time to time Maigret and Lapointe exchanged a look, and an absurd idea came into Maigret's head. How excited inwardly Antoine Batille would have been, walking among this crowd with his microphone, had he been alive. Of course, if he had been alive there would not have been any crowd.

The hearse appeared and parked at the curb, followed by three other cars. Were they going to drive to the Church of Saint-Louis-en-l'Ile, only two hundred yards away?

The undertaker's men first brought down the wreaths and sprays. Not only was the roof of the hearse covered, but the flowers filled the three cars.

Among the waiting crowd there was a third category, in little groups, the employees of Mylène Products. Lots of girls and young women, dressed with an elegance which, in the morning sunlight, had something aggressive about it.

There was a movement in the crowd like a current passing from one end of the rows to the other, and then the coffin, carried by six men, came into view. Once it had been slid into the hearse, the family appeared. At their head, Gérard Batille was flanked by his wife and daughter. His features were drawn, his complexion blotchy. He did not look at anyone but seemed surprised to see so many flowers.

One could tell that he was out of touch with reality, that he hardly noticed what was going on around him. Madame Batille showed more composure, even though at intervals she dabbed her eyes through the filmy black veil that covered her face.

Minou, the sister, whom Maigret saw for the first time in black, seemed taller and thinner, and she was the only one to pay any attention to her surroundings.

Other photographers, those of the press, took some photographs. Aunts, uncles, and relatives of varying degrees of closeness followed, and also, undoubtedly, the top ranks of the employees of the firm manufacturing perfumes and cosmetics.

The hearse moved off, the cars full of flowers, and the family fell into place behind, then the friends, students, teachers, and finally the local shopkeepers.

A certain number of those who had been standing went in the direction of the Pont-Marie or the Pont-Sully to get back to work, but there were others who went to the church.

Maigret and Lapointe were among the latter. They followed the procession along the street, and on the Rue Saint-Louis-en-l'Ile they came upon another crowd of people who had not been present on the Quai d'Anjou. The church was already more than half full. From the street one could hear the solemn murmur of the organ and the coffin was carried as far as the bier, half of which was completely covered with flowers.

Many people remained outside. The doors were not closed again and the prayers of intercession for the dead boy began while the sun and fresh air were streaming into the church.

"Pater noster . . ."

The priest, a very old man, walked around the bier shaking his aspergillum, then again swinging his censer.

"Et ne nos inducat in tentationem . . ."

"Amen. . . ."

Outside, Van Hamme was still working.

"Which cemetery?" asked Lapointe in a whisper, leaning over Maigret's shoulder.

"Montparnasse. The Batilles have a family vault there."

"Are we going there?"

"I don't think so."

Luckily, many policemen had come to direct traffic. The immediate family took their seats in the first car. The more distant relatives followed, then came Batille's colleagues, then friends who ran to get their cars and tried to thrust their way through the crowd.

Van Hamme had taken the precaution of being brought by a little black car belonging to the Criminal Police which was waiting for him at a strategic point and which took him in at the last moment.

The crowd dispersed little by little. A few groups remained talking on the sidewalks.

"We can go back," sighed Maigret.

They crossed the little bridge behind Notre Dame and stopped at a bar on the corner of the Boulevard du Palais.

"What will you have?"

"A white wine . . . Vouvray."

Because the word "Vouvray" was chalked on the windows.

"Me too. Two Vouvrays."

It was almost noon when Van Hamme came into Maigret's office, holding some prints.

"I haven't finished, but I wanted to show you something now. There are three of us studying the photographs with a strong magnifying glass. This man caught my eye at once."

The first print, on the Quai d'Anjou, only showed a part of the body and face, for there was a woman pushing from the side, forcing herself through the front row.

The man undoubtedly wore a light beige raincoat and a dark hat. He was quite young, about thirty. His face was unremarkable and he seemed to be frowning as if there was something near him that offended him.

"Here's a rather better one."

The same face, enlarged. The mouth was thickish, rather sulky, and the expression was that of a timid man.

"It's on the Quai d'Anjou too. We'll see if he appears in the photographs taken at the church. They're being developed now. I brought these down because of the raincoat."

"Weren't there any other raincoats?"

"Quite a number, but only three belted ones, one of them a middle-aged man with a beard, and one a man of about forty, hatless and smoking a pipe."

"Bring me down anything else you find after lunch."

In truth, the raincoat did not mean very much. If Batille's murderer had read the morning papers, he knew that they had published his description. Why, then, would he wear the same clothes that he had worn that evening on the Rue Popincourt? Because he had no others? As an act of defiance?

Maigret had lunch at the Brasserie Dauphine again, with Lapointe only, since Janvier and Lucas were out.

At half past two Maigret had a telephone call that made him relax a little. It seemed that suddenly a lot of his troubles were evaporating.

"Hello, Superintendent Maigret? Please hold on, our editor, Monsieur Frémiet, would like to speak to you."

"Hello, is that you, Maigret?"

The two men had known each other for many years.

Frémiet was the editor of one of the largest morning papers.

"I haven't called to see how your investigation is coming on. I'm taking the liberty of phoning you because we have just received a rather odd communication. Besides, it came by *pneumatique,* which is rare for an anonymous letter."

"Go on."

"You know we published the photographs of the members of the Jouy-en-Josas gang this morning? Under the photograph of the sailor, my writer had them print the phrase 'Is this the murderer?' "

"I saw that."

"What was sent to me was this cutting with one word, written in green ink in capital letters: NO!"

It was at that moment that Maigret's face brightened.

"If you'll let me, I'll send a rookie over for the message. Do you know which *pneumatique* office it was handed in at?"

"The Rue du Faubourg-Montmartre. May I ask you, Superintendent, not to pass the tip on to my rival editors? I can't publish the document until tomorrow morning. It has been photographed already and we're going to make a plate. . . . Unless you want us to keep it secret."

"No. On the contrary. I would even like you to comment on it. Just a minute. . . . The best thing would be if you could say you were of the opinion that it's a hoax, underlining the fact that the real murderer would not risk compromising himself in such a way."

"I think I know what you're getting at."

"Thank you, Frémiet. I'll send someone over right away."

He went into the inspectors' office, sent one of them over to the Champs-Elysées, and asked Lapointe to follow him into his office.

"You look very happy, Chief."

"Only a little! Only a little! There's still a chance that I'm wrong."

He repeated the story of the photograph cut out of the paper and the "NO" in green ink.

"I even like that green ink."

"Why?"

"Because the man who stabbed seven times, in two goes, if one can say that, in the pouring rain, while a couple are walking along the street and a woman is looking out of the window, is not quite an ordinary man.

"I've often found that people who use green ink, or red ink, have a great need to make themselves conspicuous. For them it's only one way of doing that."

"Do you mean he's a psycho?"

"I wouldn't go quite that far. Many people would say an eccentric. There are all kinds of eccentrics."

Van Hamme came into the office. This time he carried a thick bundle of photographs, some of which were still wet.

"Have you found the man in the raincoat anywhere else?"

"Except for the family and their close friends, there are only three people found in all three places, at the Quai d'Anjou, outside the church, and, finally, near the vault in the Montparnasse cemetery."

"Show me."

"First this woman."

It was a young woman, about twenty-five, with a grief-stricken face. Obviously she was troubled and

107

under great strain. She was wearing a badly cut black coat and her hair fell untidily down each side of her face.

"You told me only to pay attention to the men, but I thought . . ."

"I understand."

Maigret looked at her intently, as if to pierce her secret. She looked like a working-class girl who did not pay much attention to her outward appearance.

Why was she as moved as the members of the family, more moved than Minou, for example?

Minou had told him that her brother had probably never slept with a woman. Was she so sure about that? Couldn't she be wrong? And couldn't Antoine have had a mistress?

Given the state of mind that his search for human voices in the lowest quarters of the city revealed, was it not a girl of this type who would be likely to interest him?

"In a moment, Lapointe, when we have finished, you go back to the Ile Saint-Louis. I don't know why, but I see her as a shopgirl, in a grocer's, or perhaps a dairy. Maybe a waitress in a café or a restaurant."

"The second person," announced Van Hamme, showing an enlargement of a man of about fifty.

If his clothing had been a little more disheveled, he might have been taken for a tramp. He stared straight ahead, with a resigned look, and one wondered what there was in this funeral to interest him.

It wasn't easy to imagine him striking at a young man seven times with a knife and then running away. The murderer had not come into the area in a car, that was almost an established fact. It was more likely that he had taken the métro at the Voltaire station, close by the place where the crime had been committed. The ticket collector had only a confused memory of the occasion, for six or seven people had appeared at the entrance to the platforms in the space of one or two minutes. He punched their tickets without raising his head. It was mechanical.

"If I had to look at everyone who went by, I'd be dizzy. Heads, more heads. Faces, almost always bad-tempered."

Why had this man in the worn-out clothes stood in front of the house, then in front of the church, and why had he then gone to the Montparnasse cemetery?

"The third?" asked Maigret.

"You know him. The one I showed you this morning. You'll notice that he doesn't hide himself. He must have noticed me in all three places. Here, at the path in the cemetery, he is looking at me curiously, as if he was wondering why I was photographing the crowd and not the coffin or the family."

"That's true. He doesn't look upset or worried. Leave these photographs with me. I'm going to look at them at leisure. Thank you, Van Hamme. Tell Moers I'm very pleased with your work."

"So," asked Lapointe, once he was alone with Maigret, "I go over to the island and show people the photograph of the girl?"

"It's probably a wild-goose chase, but it's worth trying. See if Janvier is here."

He came straight into the office and looked curiously at the pile of photographs.

"Here, Janvier. I want you to go to the Sorbonne. I think you'll have no trouble at the office finding out what courses Antoine Batille went to most often."

"I'm to question his friends?"

"Exactly. Perhaps he didn't have any real friends, but he must have talked to other students.

"Here's one photograph, of a girl who appeared to be very upset at the funeral this morning and who went all the way to the cemetery. Maybe someone has seen him with her. . . . Maybe they've only heard him talk about her. . . ."

"Right."

"This photograph is of a man in a raincoat who was at the Quai d'Anjou, then at the church, and finally at the cemetery. Just in case, show it too. I hope there's a lecture this afternoon and that you'll be able to catch them coming out."

"Shall I question the lecturer?"

"I don't think they have any opportunity to know their students. But here—here's another photo. It probably has nothing to do with the case, but we'd better not overlook anything."

A quarter of an hour later Maigret was brought the newspaper cutting with the word "NO" written on it in green ink. The word had been written in capital letters almost an inch high and had been underlined with a firm stroke. The exclamation point was a good half inch higher.

It looked like an angry protest. Whoever had written those letters must have been annoyed that anyone could mistake a miserable creature like the ex-sailor for the Rue Popincourt murderer.

Maigret sat still for more than a quarter of an hour in front of the newspaper cutting and the photographs, pulling gently on his pipe. After that, almost unconsciously, he lifted up the telephone receiver.

"Hello, Frémiet? I was afraid you might not still be

there. Thank you for the document, which looks very interesting to me. I thought at first I'd put an advertisement in the personal column in tomorrow morning's paper, but he may not read the personal column.

"You'll undoubtedly have an article on the case. . . ."

"Our reporters are studying the previous burglaries. I have them working in a radius of thirty miles from Paris, showing photographs of the gang to all the neighbors of the houses that were robbed."

"Could you put the following lines below the article, or articles?

" 'Superintendent Maigret would like to know on what the man who sent the *pneumatique* to the newspaper bases his statement. He begs him to be so good as to get in touch with him, either by letter or by telephone, if he has any interesting information.' "

"I understand. Could you repeat that, so that I can be sure I've got every word?"

Maigret repeated it patiently.

"Right. Not only will I print this announcement on the front page, I'll put it in a box. You must know you'll get letters or phone calls from madmen."

Maigret smiled.

"I'm used to that. You must be too, of course. Policemen and newspaper editors."

"Good. Thank you for keeping me up to date."

And the superintendent immersed himself in the evening papers that had just been brought to him, groaning each time he found a new error. There was an average of one, or at least an exaggeration, per paragraph, and the picture thieves had become one of the most mysterious and best-organized gangs in Paris.

The final headline:

"WHEN WILL THEY ARREST
THE BRAIN?"

Just like the T.V. serials.

He had sent the article and the photograph of the
sailor with the "NO" in green letters to the criminal
anthropometry department so that they could get any
fingerprints from it. The answer came back quickly.

"A thumbprint on the photograph, and a very good
index finger on the back of the paper. These prints do
not tally with any prints in the records."

That meant, obviously, that Antoine Batille's murderer had never been arrested and, even more, that he
had no convictions.

Maigret was not at all surprised and he was just
about to start reading the papers again when Lapointe
burst in, very excited.

"Some people get it with jam on, Chief! I mean,
what luck! And you were right. I was going across the
footbridge and I found I had no more cigarettes. So I
went to the Rue Saint-Louis-en-l'Ile. I went into the
tobacco shop on the corner and who did I see?"

"The girl whose picture I gave you."

"Exactly. She's a waitress there. Wears a black dress
and a white apron. There was one table of belote
players —the butcher, the grocer, the proprietor, and a
man who had his back to me. I picked up my cigarettes and went over and sat down.

"When she asked me what I wanted to drink, I ordered a coffee and she went and made me an espresso at
the counter.

" 'When do you close in the evenings?'

"She looked a bit surprised.

" 'That depends on the evening. I finish at seven be-cause it's me who opens in the mornings.'

"She gave me my change and went off without pay-ing any more attention to me. I decided not to speak to her in front of her boss. I thought you'd rather do it yourself."

"You were right."

"She always seemed on the point of tears. She walked about in a fog and her nose is red."

Janvier didn't come back to the Quai until six o'clock.

"There was a sociology lecture and it seems he never cut that one. I waited in the courtyard. I watched the students sitting on their benches and then, when the lecture was over, they rushed outside.

"I buttonholed two or three without success.

" 'Antoine Batille? The fellow the papers are talking about? I've seen him, yes, but we never spoke to each other. If you could possibly find a fellow called Harteau . . .'

"The third student I collared looked around, called suddenly, turning to a young man who was moving off:

" 'Harteau! Harteau! This man wants to talk to you.'

"And then said to me:

" 'I must go. I have to catch a train.'

"Other students were going off on scooters and mo-torbikes.

" 'Did you want to speak to me?' asked a tall young man with a pale face and light gray eyes.

" 'I understand you were Antoine Batille's friend.'

" 'Friend is saying a lot. He didn't make friends eas-ily. Let's say we knew each other and we sometimes talked out here in the courtyard and had a beer together from time to time. I only went to his house once and I didn't feel at ease. You see, my mother's a concierge on the Place Denfert-Rochereau. I'm not ashamed of it. But I didn't know how I ought to behave there.'

" 'Were you at the funeral this morning?'

" 'Only at the church. After that I had an important lecture.'

" 'Do you know if your friend had any enemies?'

" 'He certainly didn't have any.'

" 'Was he well liked?'

" 'He wasn't well liked either. People didn't pay any attention to him any more than he did to them.'

" 'What about you? What did you think about him?'

" 'He was a nice fellow. He was much more sensitive than he let on. I think he was too sensitive and he closed up easily.'

" 'Did he ever talk to you about his tape recorder?'

" 'One day he asked me to go with him. He was crazy about it. He said that people's voices are more revealing than their photographs. I remember something he said:

" ' "There are plenty of picture hunters. I don't know any other sound hunters."

" 'He hoped to get one of the latest miniature microphones from Japan for Christmas. You can hold them in the palm of your hand. They aren't available in France yet, but it seems they're waiting for them to come in. He could only have known about them through magazine articles.' "

Janvier had not forgotten to ask Harteau if Batille had a mistress.

" 'A mistress, no. At least, not as far as I know. He

wasn't the type. Besides, he was shy, reserved. And he had fallen in love a few weeks ago.

"'He couldn't help telling me. He had to tell someone, and his sister usually laughed at him and said he was the girl of the family and she was the boy. . . .

"'I never saw the girl, but she works on the Ile Saint-Louis and he saw her every morning at eight o'clock. That's when she was alone in the café. The proprietor was still asleep and his wife was doing the housework upstairs.

"'They were interrupted incessantly by customers, but they still had some time alone together.'

"'Was it really serious?'

"'I think so.'

"'What were his intentions?'

"'In what way?'

"'How did he see his future, for example?'

"'He wanted to take anthropology next year. His dream was to be a teacher in Asia, in Africa, in South America, one after the other, so that he could study the different races. He wanted to prove that they are basically the same, that the differences between them will disappear when living conditions are the same everywhere.'

"'Did he mean to get married?'

"'He hadn't spoken about that yet. It had happened too recently. In any case, he didn't want to marry a girl with the same background as his.'

"'Did he rebel against his parents, against his family?'

"'Not even that. I remember he once said to me:

"' "When I go home, it's like living in 1900." '

"'Thank you. I'm sorry for taking so much of your time.'"

115

And Janvier concluded:

"What do you think, Chief? If the girl had a brother . . . If they'd gone further than Harteau thinks . . . If the brother took it into his head that the son of Mylène perfumes would never marry his sister . . . You see what I mean?"

"Now you're getting a bit 1900, aren't you, Janvier?"

"It still happens, doesn't it?"

"Haven't you read the statistics? So-called crimes of passion have dropped by more than half, so much so that they seem like a delightful anachronism.

"In fact, Lapointe has found her and she does work on the Ile Saint-Louis. I'm going to try to talk to her this evening."

"What do I do now?"

"Nothing. Anything. We're waiting."

At a quarter past six, Maigret had a drink in the Brasserie Dauphine, where he met two of his colleagues. At the Quai they often went for weeks without seeing each other, each one being almost shut up in his own branch. The Brasserie Dauphine was the neutral territory where everyone saw everyone else at last.

"Well, what about the Rue Popincourt murder? Are you working for the Rue des Saussaies now?"

At ten minutes to seven, Maigret walked the short distance to the Rue Saint-Louis-en-l'Ile, and he could see the girl serving the customers in the tobacco shop.

The proprietor's wife was at the cash desk, the proprietor serving behind the bar. It was the short rush hour of the early evening.

At five minutes past seven the girl went through a door and reappeared some moments later wearing the coat that he had seen in the photograph. She said a few

116

words to the proprietor's wife and came out. She turned right in the direction of the Quai d'Anjou without looking around, and Maigret had to quicken his pace to catch up with her.

"Excuse me, Mademoiselle. . . ."

She mistook his intentions and was on the point of running.

"I am Superintendent Maigret. I wanted to talk to you about Antoine."

She stopped short and looked at him with a sort of anguish.

"What did you say?"

"That I want to talk to you about . . ."

"I heard you. But I don't understand. I don't . . ."

"There's no point in denying it, Mademoiselle."

"Who told you?"

"Your photograph, or rather your photographs. You were outside the house this morning, holding a handkerchief in your clenched fists. You were at the church when the funeral party went in and when it came out, and after that you were at the cemetery."

"Why was I photographed?"

"If you would spare me a few minutes and walk along with me, I'll explain it to you. We are looking for Antoine Batille's killer. We haven't any real trail to follow, no useful clue. . . .

"In the hope that the murderer would be drawn to the funeral of his victim I had photographs taken of the rows of the curious. The photographer then looked for the people who were to be found at the Quai d'Anjou, at the church, and at the cemetery."

She bit her lip. They were walking quite naturally along the embankment and they passed in front of the Batilles' place. The black hangings with their silver

117

teardrops had disappeared. There were lights on all floors. The house had resumed its normal rhythm of life.

"What do you want of me?"

"I want you to tell me all you know about Antoine. You are the person who was closest to him."

She blushed suddenly.

"What makes you say that?"

"He was the one who said it, in a way. He had a friend at the Sorbonne . . ."

"The concierge's son?"

"Yes."

"He was his only friend. He didn't feel at ease with the others. He always felt he was different."

"Well, he led this Harteau to understand that he intended to marry you one day."

"Are you sure he said that?"

"Didn't he say so to you?"

"No. I wouldn't have accepted. We don't belong to the same world. . . ."

"Perhaps he didn't belong to any world except his own."

"Besides, his family . . ."

"How long had he known you?"

"Ever since I've worked at the tobacco shop. That's four months. It was winter, I remember. It was snowing the first day I saw him. He was buying a pack of Gitanes. He bought one every day."

"How long was it before he waited for you to come out?"

"More than a month."

"Did you become his mistress?"

"Just a week ago today."

"Have you a brother?"

"I have two. One is in the army, in Germany, the other one works in Lyons."

"Do you come from Lyons?"

"My father came from there. Now that he's dead, the family has scattered and I'm alone in Paris with my mother. We live on the Rue Saint-Paul. I used to work in a department store, but I couldn't stand it. It was too tiring for me. When I learned they were looking for a waitress on the Rue Saint-Louis-en-l'Ile . . ."

"Did Antoine have any enemies?"

"Why would he have had any enemies?"

"His passion for taking his tape recorder into certain places with bad reputations."

"No one paid any attention to him. He sat in a corner or stood at the bar. He took me with him twice."

"Did you meet every evening?"

"He came to meet me at the shop and took me home. Once or twice a week we went to the movies."

"Will you tell me your name?"

"Mauricette."

"Mauricette what?"

"Mauricette Gallois."

They had retraced their steps slowly, crossed the Pont Sainte-Marie, and they were now on the Rue Saint-Paul.

"This is where I live. Have you anything else to ask me?"

"Not at the moment. Thank you very much, Mauricette. Don't lose heart."

Maigret sighed and, outside the Saint-Paul métro station, took a taxi that got him home in a few minutes. He forced himself not to think about his case and, after turning the television on, out of habit, he turned it off for fear it would still be talking about the Rue Popincourt and the picture thieves.

"What are you thinking?"

"That we're going to the movies and that it's almost warm this evening. We can walk as far as the Grands Boulevards."

It was one of his most unfailing pleasures. After a few steps, Madame Maigret would take his arm and they would walk along slowly, stopping sometimes to look at a shop-window. They didn't keep up a continuous conversation but chatted about this and that, about a passing face, a dress, the last letter from his sister-in-law.

That evening Maigret wanted to see a Western and they had to go as far as the Porte Saint-Denis to find one. In the intermission he treated himself to a glass of calvados and his wife had a verbena tisane.

At midnight they put out the lights in their apartment. The next day was a Saturday, the 22nd of March. The previous evening it had not occurred to Maigret that it was the first day of spring. It was on time this year. He saw again in his mind's eye the morning light on the Quai d'Anjou, outside the house where the boy's body lay.

At nine o'clock he had a telephone call from Magistrate Poiret.

"Anything new, Maigret?"

"Not yet, Magistrate. At any rate, nothing definite."

"You don't think that that sailor, what's his name again? . . . Yvon Demarle . . ."

"I'm sure that although he may be in up to his ears in the picture thefts, he has nothing to do with the Rue Popincourt murder."

"Have you any idea?"

"It's beginning to get a bit clearer. It's too vague for me to tell you about it, but I'm waiting for certain developments to take place in a very short time."

"A crime of passion?"

"I don't think so."

"A sex crime?"

He hated such classifications.

"I don't think so."

He did not have to wait long before learning something new. The telephone rang half an hour later. It was the chief reporter of one of the evening papers.

"Superintendent Maigret? Jean Rolland here. I'm not disturbing you, am I? Don't worry, I'm not calling you for information, though if you have any it's always welcome."

Maigret was not on especially good terms with the editor of that particular paper, precisely because he was always complaining that he was not told about important things before anyone else.

"Our circulation is as big as three other papers put together. It would be only natural . . ."

It wasn't a quarrel between them, more a kind of strained relationship. That was probably why the chief reporter was telephoning and not the editor.

"Did you read our stories yesterday?"

"I looked through them."

"We tried to analyze the possibility of a connection between the two cases. In the end we found as many points for as against. . . ."

"I know."

"Well, one story brought us in a letter in this morning's mail, which I'm going to read to you. . . ."

"Just a moment. Is the address written in block letters?"

"That's right. The letter is too."

"I suppose it's written on ordinary paper like what's sold in packs of six tablets in tobacconists' and grocers'."

"Right again. Did you get a letter too?"

"No. Go on."

"Here it is:

"*Dear Editor,*

"*I have read carefully the stories printed in the last few days in your worthy paper on the subject of what is called the Rue Popincourt Case and the Paintings Case. Your writer tries, without any success, to establish a link between these two cases.*

"*I find it naïve on the part of the press to think that young Batille was attacked on the Rue Popincourt because of a tape recording. Besides, did the killer take his tape recorder away?*

"*As for the sailor Demarle, he has never killed anyone with his Swedish knife.*

"*These knives are sold in all good hardware stores, and I have one too.*

"*But mine really did kill Antoine Batille. I am not boasting, believe me. I am not proud of it. Quite the contrary. But all this fuss tires me. And above all I would not like an innocent man like Demarle to pay for my crime.*

"*You may publish this letter if you see fit. I guarantee that it is the truth.*

"*Thank you. Yours very sincerely.'*"

Of course there was no signature.

"Do you think it's a joke, Superintendent?"

"No."

"Can it be serious?"

"I'm sure it is. Of course, I may be wrong, but there's every chance that this letter was written by the murderer. Look at the postmark and tell me where it was posted."

"Boulevard Saint-Michel."

"You may have it photographed in case you want to print a copy of it, but I would like it to be handled as little as possible."

"Do you expect to find fingerprints?"

"I'm almost sure I'll find some."

"Were there any on the newspaper cutting with the NO written on it in green ink?"

"Yes."

"I read your appeal. Are you hoping the killer will telephone you?"

"If he's the kind of man I think he is, he will."

"I suppose there's no point in asking you what kind of man you mean?"

"That's right. At the moment I can say nothing. I'll send someone over to you to pick up the letter and I'll give it back to you as soon as the case is over."

"Fine. Good luck."

Maigret turned toward the door, astonished. Joseph, the old usher, was framed in the doorway and behind him stood a man in a beige uniform with wide brown stripes down the sides of his trousers. His cap was beige too and bore a coat of arms with a golden crown.

"What is this?" the superintendent asked the intruder.

"I have a message from Monsieur Lherbier."

"The leather merchant?"

"Yes."

"Are you waiting for a reply?"

"I was not told to, but I was ordered to put this parcel into your own hands. Monsieur Lherbier himself told me to do it, late yesterday afternoon."

Maigret had unwrapped a beige cardboard box marked with the ubiquitous crown, and in this box he discovered a black crocodile wallet the corners of which were reinforced with gold. The crown was gold too.

A visiting card bore simply the words:

"A token of my gratitude."

The superintendent put the wallet back into its box.

"One moment," he said to the man who had brought it. "You will probably be more efficient than I would at retying the parcel."

The man stared at him, surprised.

"Don't you like it?"

"Tell your employer that I never accept gifts. You may add, if you wish, that nevertheless I appreciate the gesture."

"Won't you write to him?"

"No."

The telephone rang insistently.

"Here, take it. Go and do up the package in the waiting room. I'm very busy."

And, when he was alone at last, he picked up the receiver.

Chapter **6**   "It's someone who won't give his name, Superintendent. Shall I put him through to you anyway? He says you know who he is."

"Put him through."

He heard the click and said hello in a voice that was not quite his normal voice.

And, after a moment of silence, a speaker who seemed very far away repeated, like an echo: "Hello."

They were both very nervous, and Maigret made himself a promise to avoid saying anything that might frighten away the man he was speaking to.

"Do you know who this is talking to you?"

"Yes."

"Do you know my name?"

"Your name is of no importance."

"Aren't you going to try to find out where I'm calling you from?"

The tone was hesitant. The man lacked assurance and was trying to bolster up his courage.

"No."

"Why not?"

"Because I'm not interested in that."

"Don't you believe me?"

"Yes, I do."

"You believe that I'm the Rue Popincourt man?"

"Yes."

This time there was quite a long silence, then the voice, shy and worried, asked:

"Are you still there?"

"Yes. I'm listening."

"Has anyone brought you the letter I wrote to the paper yet?"

"No. It was read to me over the telephone."

"Have you got the clipping with the photograph?"

"Yes."

"You do believe me? You don't think I am mad?"

"I've already told you so."

"What do you think of me?"

"First of all, I know that you have never been convicted of any crime."

"Because of my fingerprints?"

"Exactly. You are accustomed to leading a quiet, orderly life."

"How did you guess that?"

Maigret did not say anything and the other man panicked again.

"Don't hang up."

"Do you have a lot to tell me?"

"I don't know. Perhaps. I have nobody to talk to."

"You aren't married, are you?"

"No."

"You live alone. You've taken the day off today, perhaps by calling your office and telling them that you're ill."

"You're trying to make me say things that will help you to trap me. Are you sure that some of your technicians aren't trying to find out where I'm speaking to you from?"

"I give you my word on that."

"So you aren't in a hurry to arrest me?"

"I'm like you. I'm glad it's all over."

"How do you know?"

"You have written to the papers."

"I didn't want anyone to accuse an innocent man."

"That wasn't the real reason."

"Do you imagine that I'm trying to be caught?"

"Subconsciously, yes."

"What else do you think about me?"

"You feel lost."

"The truth is, I'm afraid."

"What are you afraid of? Being arrested?"

"No. It doesn't matter. I've already said too much. I wanted to talk to you and to hear your voice. Do you despise me?"

"I don't despise anyone."

"Not even a criminal?"

"Not even a criminal."

"You know you'll get me one of these days, don't you?"

"Yes."

"Do you have any clues to my identity?"

Maigret almost told him, to get it over with, that he already had his photograph, first at the Quai d'Anjou, then in front of the church, and finally at the Montparnasse cemetery.

He only had to have those pictures printed in the newspapers for a number of people to tell him the identity of Batille's murderer.

If he did not do it, it was because he had a hazy idea that in this particular case the man would not wait to be arrested and it would certainly be a dead body that would be found at his home.

It had to come from within himself, slowly.

"There are always clues, but it's difficult to assess their worth."

"I'm going to hang up soon."

"What are you going to do today?"

"What do you mean?"

"It's Saturday. Are you going to spend Sunday in the country?"

"Of course not."

"Don't you have a car?"

"No."

"You work in an office, don't you?"

"That's right. There are tens of thousands of offices in Paris, so I can tell you that."

"Have you any friends?"

"No."

"A girl friend?"

"No. When I need one, I make do with what I find. You know what I mean?"

"I think that when tomorrow comes you'll spend the day writing a long letter to the papers."

"How do you manage to know everything?"

"Because you aren't the first person to be in this situation."

"And how did it end up for the others?"

"There have been different endings."

"Did any of them kill themselves?"

Maigret did not answer, and silence reigned once again on the line.

"I don't have a revolver and I know that it's almost impossible to get one now without a special permit."

"You won't commit suicide."

"What makes you think that?"

"You wouldn't have telephoned me."

Maigret wiped his forehead. This conversation, apparently so commonplace, these flat answers, allowed him none the less to pin down the character of the man more and more.

"I'm going to hang up," said the voice at the end of the line.

"You can call me again on Monday."

"Not tomorrow?"

"Tomorrow's Sunday and I shan't be in my office."

"Won't you be at home?"

"I'm planning to go to the country with my wife."

Each sentence was carefully planned.

"You're lucky."

"Yes."

"Are you happy?"

"Relatively so, like most men."

"I've never been happy."

He hung up suddenly. Either someone, impatient at seeing him talk for so long, had tried to get into the phone booth, or the dialogue had laid his nerves bare.

He wasn't a drinking man. Perhaps he might make an exception, to brace himself. He had phoned from a café or a bar. People would be elbowing him, looking at him without imagining he was a killer.

Maigret telephoned his wife.

"What would you say to spending the weekend at Meung-sur-Loire?"

She was so surprised that for a moment she could not speak.

"But . . . you . . . What about your case?"

"It needs to simmer for a bit."

"When shall we go?"

"After lunch."

"In the car?"

"Of course."

She had been driving for a year, but she was not yet easy about it and she always gripped the wheel with an unconquerable apprehension.

"Buy something for this evening's dinner, because we may get there after the shops shut. Get something to make a big breakfast tomorrow morning too. We'll have lunch at the inn."

He didn't find any of the men he worked most closely with except Janvier, and he invited him for a drink.

"What are you doing tomorrow?"

"You know, Chief, that Sunday is the day for my mother-in-law and the children's uncles and aunts."

"We're going to Meung."

He and his wife had a quick lunch at home on the Boulevard Richard-Lenoir. Then, when the dishes were done, Madame Maigret went to change.

"Is it cold?"

"A bit cool."

"So I can't wear my flowered dress?"

"Why not? You're taking a coat, aren't you?"

An hour later they joined the flow of tens of thousands of Parisians who were rushing to find a patch of green.

They found the house as clean and tidy as if they had left it the day before, for a local woman came in twice a week to air the house, dust it, and do the floors. It was useless to tell her about new housekeeping aids. Everything was freshly waxed, including the furniture, and a pleasant smell of polish pervaded everything.

Her husband took care of the garden, and Maigret found crocuses on the lawn and, at the foot of the little wall at the end of the garden, in the most sheltered spot, jonquils and tulips.

His first act was to go upstairs and put on an old pair of trousers and a flannel shirt. He always had the feeling that the house, with its bare beams and its dark corners, with the peace that pervaded it, was like a priest's house. That did not displease him—quite the contrary.

Madame Maigret busied herself in the kitchen.

"Are you very hungry?"

"Just ordinarily hungry."

They had no television here. After dinner, when the weather was a little warmer, they sat in the garden and watched the twilight close in little by little, blotting out the features of the landscape.

That evening they went for a leisurely walk, going as far as the Loire, whose water, after the rains at the beginning of the week, flowed muddily and carried the branches of trees along with it.

"Are you worried?"

He did not speak for some time.

"Not really. Antoine Batille's killer called me up this morning."

"Out of cheek? Or defiance?"

"No. He needed reassurance."

"And he turned to you?"

"There wasn't anyone else he could use."

"Are you sure it's the murderer?"

"I said the killer. A murder assumes premeditation."

"His act was not premeditated?"

"Not exactly, unless I'm mistaken."

"Why did he write to the papers?"

"You've read his letter?"

"Yes. I thought at first it was a joke. Do you know who he is?"

"No, but I could find out within twenty-four hours."

"Don't you want to arrest him?"

"He'll give himself up of his own accord."

"And if he doesn't give himself up? If he commits another crime?"

"I don't think that . . ."

But the superintendent stopped himself as if in doubt.

Had he the right to be so sure of himself? He thought of Antoine Batille, who dreamed of going to study tropical man and who wanted to marry young Mauricette.

He wasn't yet twenty-one and he had been struck down in a puddle on the Rue Popincourt, never to get up again.

Maigret slept fitfully. He opened his eyes twice, thinking he heard the telephone ring.

"He won't kill again."

He tried to reassure himself.

"After all, it's himself he's afraid of."

A real Sunday sun, a sun like those we remember from childhood. The garden, covered with dew, smelled good and the house smelled of bacon and eggs.

The day passed uneventfully. Nevertheless Maigret's expression was withdrawn. He did not manage to relax completely and his wife sensed it.

They were welcomed at the inn with open arms and they had to have a drink with everyone, for they were considered almost as belonging there.

"A game of cards, this afternoon?"

Why not? They ate rillettes done in the local way, *coq au vin blanc,* and, after the goat cheese, *babas au rhum.*

"About four o'clock?"

"Fine."

He took his wicker chair to the most sheltered spot in the garden and fell asleep before long with the sunlight warming his eyelids.

When he woke up, Madame Maigret made him a cup of coffee.

"You were sleeping so soundly it was a real pleasure to watch you."

He still had a sort of country taste in his mouth and

132

he imagined he could hear flies still buzzing around him.

"Didn't it give you a funny feeling listening to his voice on the telephone?"

They were both thinking about it, in spite of themselves, each one in a different way.

"After forty years in this job, I'm always affected when I meet a man who has killed."

"Why?"

"Because he has crossed the barrier."

He did not explain any more. He knew what he meant. The man who kills cuts himself off, as it were, from human society. From one minute to the next he ceases to be a man like other men.

He wanted to explain himself, to say . . . Quantities of words rose to his lips but he knew there was no point, no one would understand him.

Even the real killers, the professionals. They looked aggressive, sardonic; it was because they needed to swagger, to make themselves believe that they still existed as men.

"You won't be coming back very late?"

"I expect to be back before six thirty."

He joined his local friends, good men for whom he was not the famous Superintendent Maigret but a neighbor and, moreover, an excellent fisherman. The red cloth was spread out in front of them. The cards, which had seen better days, were a bit sticky. The white local wine was cool and sparkling.

"Your call."

"Diamonds."

His opponent on the left announced a sequence of three, his partner four queens.

"Trump."

The afternoon went in dealing cards, in arranging them in fans, in announcing tierces or bellas. It was like a peaceful droning. From time to time the landlord would come over to have a look at each man's hand and would go off again with a knowing smile.

Sunday must be seeming long to the man who had killed Antoine Batille. Maigret hoped he had not stayed at home. Did he have a little apartment, with his own furniture, or did he rent a room by the month in a cheap hotel?

It would be better for him not to stay between four walls but to go out and rub shoulders with the crowd or go to the movies.

On that Tuesday evening on the Rue Popincourt it had been raining so hard that it was practically a cataclysm and elsewhere, in the Channel and in the North Sea, fishing boats had gone down.

Maigret tried not to think about it, to keep his mind on the game.

"Well, Superintendent, what do you say?"

"I pass."

The white wine was going to his head a little. He wasn't used to it any more. One drank it like water and only afterward felt the effects.

"I'll have to go soon."

"We'll stop at five hundred points, all right?"

"Five hundred points is fine."

He lost and paid for the drinks.

"One can see that you don't play belote in Paris. You're out of practice, aren't you?"

"Yes, a bit."

"You'll have to come and stay a little longer at Easter."

"I hope to. There's nothing I'd like better. It's the villains who . . ."

And there he was! Suddenly he was thinking about the telephone again.

"Good evening, gentlemen."

"Shall we see you next Saturday?"

"Maybe."

He did not feel let down. He had had the weekend away which he had made up his mind to have, but he couldn't expect that his worries and responsibilities would not follow him into the country.

"When do you want to leave?"

"As soon as we've had a little something to eat. What have you got for dinner?"

"Old Bambois came and offered me a tench, and I baked it."

He went and looked greedily at the swollen skin, a beautiful golden color.

They drove slowly, since Madame Maigret was even more nervous at night than in the daytime. Maigret turned on the radio and smiled as he listened to the warnings to drivers and then to the news.

It was mostly about foreign politics, and the superintendent gave a sigh of relief on discovering that there was no mention of the Rue Popincourt case.

In other words, the killer had behaved himself. No crimes. No suicides. Only a little girl kidnapped in Bouches-du-Rhône. They were hoping to find her alive.

He slept better than he had the previous night, and it was broad daylight when a truck whose exhaust seemed about to split wide open woke him up. His wife was not lying beside him.

She must just have got up, for her part of the bed was still warm and she was busy in the kitchen making the coffee.

———

Leaning over the banister, Madame Maigret watched him walk heavily downstairs, somewhat as she would have watched a child going off to take a difficult examination. She knew hardly any more than the papers did, but what the papers did not know was with what energy he tried to understand, how much concentration he had to have over certain cases. It seemed as though he identified himself with the people he was hunting down and that he went through their anguish with them.

By chance he found a bus with an open platform and so could go on smoking his first pipe of the morning. He had hardly arrived at his office when Superintendent Grosjean telephoned him.

"How's it going, Maigret?"

"Very well. What about you? What's the news of your burglars?"

"Contrary to what one might think, it's Gouvion, the poor little lookout, who's being most useful to us and who has enabled us to find witnesses for two of the burglaries, one at the Château de l'Epine, near Arpajon, and the other at a villa in the Forest of Dreux.

"Gouvion often stayed at his post for three or four days, watching the comings and goings. He would go and have a bite to eat or a drink in the neighborhood.

"I think he'll break before long and he'll talk. His wife, who used to be a dancer at the Châtelet, is begging him to.

"All four of them are at the Santé, in separate cells.

"I wanted to keep you up to date and to thank you again. What about your case?"

"It's coming along slowly."

Half an hour later, as he expected, the editor of the morning paper wanted to speak to him.

"Another letter?"

"Yes, except this one didn't come in the mail but was shoved into our letter box."

"A long letter?"

"Long enough. The envelope says 'For the attention of the writer of Saturday's piece on the Rue Popincourt crime.'"

"Still in block letters?"

"He seems to write that way very easily. Shall I read it to you?"

"Please."

"'Dear Sir,

"'I have read your latest stories, Saturday's in particular, and although I am not able to judge their literary value, I have the impression that you are really looking for the truth. Some of your colleagues are not of the same mind and, ever on the hunt for the sensational, print anything, even if they contradict themselves the next day.

"'I have, however, one complaint to make to you. In your last piece you speak of "the madman of the Rue Popincourt." Why this word, which first of all is hurtful and secondly makes a judgment? Because there were seven stabs? No doubt, so you could say a little further on that the murderer struck like a madman.

"'Do you know that you can do a lot of harm by using words of that kind? Certain situations are painful enough in themselves not to be judged in a superficial manner.

"'I do not ask to be treated with kid gloves. I know that in everyone's eyes I am a killer. But I would prefer not to be annoyed, to boot, by words that are probably stronger than the intention of those who use them.

"'Apart from that, I must thank you for your objectivity.

"'I can tell you that I have telephoned Superintendent

137

Maigret. He seemed to me to be very understanding and I want to trust him. But how far does his profession oblige him to play a part, let alone set traps?

"'*I think I shall telephone him again. I feel very tired. Tomorrow, however, I shall go back to work.*

"'*On Saturday I went to Antoine Batille's funeral. I saw his father, his mother, and his sister. I want them to know that I had nothing against their son. I didn't even know him. I had never seen him before. I am truly sorry for the evil I have done them.*

"'*Yours very sincerely.*'

"Shall I print it?"

"I don't see why not. In fact, it will encourage him to write again and in each letter he tells us a little more about himself. When you have had it photographed, send it to me. There's no need to send a messenger."

The phone call did not come until ten minutes past twelve, when Maigret was wondering whether to go for lunch.

"I suppose you're calling me from a café or a bar near your office?"

"That's right. Were you waiting for me?"

"I was just going out for lunch."

"Didn't you know I would telephone?"

"Yes, I did."

"Have you read my letter? I expect they read them to you over the telephone. That's why I don't send you a copy."

"You need people to read you, don't you?"

"I don't want them to get mistaken ideas. Just because someone has killed, people make assumptions about him. You too, I expect."

"Well, you know, I've known many of them."

"I know."

"When we used to send convicts abroad to prison islands, some men wrote to me from Guiana. Others, when they've served their time, come and see me sometimes."

"Really?"

"Do you feel any better?"

"I don't know. Anyway, I was able to work almost normally this morning. It makes me laugh to think that those same people who are so natural with me would be quite different if I only said one little sentence."

"Do you want to say it?"

"There are moments when I have to hold myself in. With my boss, for example, who looks down on me from a great height."

"Were you born in Paris?"

"No. In a little town in the provinces. I won't tell you which, because that would help you to identify me."

"What did your father do?"

"He's head accountant in a . . . let's say, in a fairly big firm. The man who can be trusted, you know the type. The fool the bosses can keep at work until ten in the evening and make him come in on Saturday afternoons, not to mention Sundays."

"What about your mother?"

"She's an invalid. As far back as I can remember, I can see her always ill. It seems it was caused by my birth."

"You haven't any brothers or sisters?"

"No. That's why. She does her own housework, though, and keeps the house very clean. When I was at school I was one of the cleanest pupils, too.

"My parents are proud people. They wanted me to be a lawyer, or a doctor. But I'd had enough of studying. So then they thought I would go into the firm where my father works, which is the biggest employer in the town. I didn't want to stay there. I felt I was suffocating. I came to Paris . . ."

"Where you suffocate in an office, don't you?"

"But when I leave it at the end of the day nobody knows me. I'm free."

He was talking more easily, more naturally, than the previous time. He was less afraid. His silences were less frequent.

"What do you think of me?"

"Haven't you asked me that already?"

"I mean me in general. Forgetting the Rue Popincourt."

"I think you're one of tens, of hundreds of thousands, in the same situation."

"Most of them are married and have children."

"Why have you never married? Because of your . . . illness?"

"Do you really think the things you're saying?"

"Yes."

"Every word?"

"Yes."

"I can't understand you. You aren't at all what I imagined a superintendent in the Criminal Police would be like."

"A superintendent is like anyone else. Even at the Quai des Orfèvres, we're all different from each other."

"What I don't understand most of all is what you said to me the last time. You said that it would take you twenty-four hours to identify me."

"That's right."

"How?"

"I'll tell you that when I see you."

"What is your reason for not doing it and not arresting me right away?"

"Suppose I were to ask you what was your reason for killing?"

There was a silence, more notable than the others, and the superintendent wondered if he had not gone too far.

"Hello," he called.

"Yes."

"I'm sorry I was so brutal. You have to look things right in the eye."

"I know. That's what I'm trying to do, believe me. Maybe you think I write to the papers and telephone you because I need to talk about myself. Really it's because everything is so wrong."

"What is wrong?"

"What people think. The questions they'll ask me in court, if I ever get there. The Public Prosecutor's charge and even, perhaps most of all, my lawyer's defense."

"You're thinking so far ahead already?"

"I have to."

"Do you expect to be giving yourself up?"

"You think I will, soon, don't you?"

"Yes."

"Do you think I'll feel better for it?"

"I'm sure you will."

"I'll be shut in a cell and treated like a . . ."

He did not finish his sentence and Maigret did not interrupt him.

"I don't want to keep you any longer. Your wife will be waiting for you."

"She certainly won't be worried. She's used to it."

Another silence. It seemed as though he did not want to cut the thread that linked him to another man.

"Are you happy?" he asked shyly, as if that question obsessed him.

"Relatively happy. That is, as happy as anyone can be."

"I've never been happy since I was fourteen, not for one day, not for an hour, not even for a minute."

Suddenly he changed his tone.

"Thank you."

And he hung up.

The superintendent had to go up to Magistrate Poiret's office in the afternoon.

"Are you making any progress with your investigations?" the magistrate asked with the touch of impatience common to all magistrates.

"It is almost over."

"Does that mean that you know who the murderer is?"

"He telephoned me again this morning."

"Who is he?"

From his pocket Maigret took the enlargement of a head photographed among the crowd in the sunshine on the Quai d'Anjou.

"That young man?"

"He's not as young as all that. He's in his thirties."

"Have you arrested him?"

"Not yet."

"Where does he live?"

"I don't know his name or his address. If I have this photograph printed, people who see him every day, his colleagues, his concierge, anyone, would recognize him and wouldn't hesitate to tell me who he is."

"Why don't you do it?"

"That's the question that's worrying him too and which he asked me this morning for the second time."

"Had he phoned you before?"

"Yes, on Saturday."

142

"You realize, Superintendent, the responsibility you are taking on yourself? A responsibility, moreover, which I share indirectly, now that I have seen the photograph. I don't like that."

"I don't, either. But if I moved too quickly he probably wouldn't let himself be arrested but would prefer to bring things to a conclusion."

"You are afraid he may commit suicide?"

"He has nothing else to lose. Don't you agree?"

"Hundreds of criminals have been caught and the number of them who have attempted to end their lives . . ."

"And what if he is precisely one of those?"

"Has he written to the papers?"

"A letter was put in the letter box of one newspaper office, yesterday evening or in the small hours this morning."

"That is a well-known pattern, I think. If I remember my courses in criminology correctly, that is usually the way with paranoiacs."

"Yes, according to the psychiatrists."

"Don't you agree with them?"

"I don't know enough about it to contradict them. The only difference between them and me is that I don't divide people into categories."

"It is necessary, however."

"Why is it necessary?"

"In order to pass judgment, for example."

"It is not my place to pass judgment."

"They were right to warn me that you were difficult to manage."

The magistrate said it with a slight smile, but he meant it, nevertheless.

"Would you agree to a bargain? It is Monday now. Shall we say that if on Wednesday at the same time . . ."

"Go on."

"If your man isn't under lock and key by then, you will send his photograph to the papers?"

"Would you really stick to that?"

"I'm letting you have a delay that I consider to be sufficient."

"Thank you."

Maigret went back down to his own floor and opened the door of the inspectors' office. He didn't particularly need them.

"Are you coming, Janvier?"

Once in his office, he went over to open the window, for he was hot, and the noises from outside thundered into the room. He sat down at his desk and picked up a curved pipe that he smoked less frequently than the others.

"Anything new?"

"Nothing new, Chief."

"Sit down."

The magistrate had not understood a thing. For him, criminals were defined by this or that article of the penal code.

Maigret too sometimes needed to think aloud.

"He called me again."

"He hasn't decided to give himself up?"

"He wants to. He's still hesitating, as one might hesitate to jump into icy water."

"I suppose he trusts you."

"I think so. But he knows I'm not on my own. I've just come down from upstairs. When the magistrate begins to question him he will unfortunately have to take notice of some realities.

"I know a little more about him. He comes from a small town in the provinces, he didn't want to tell me which one. That means that it's a very small town, where we would have no difficulty in picking up his trail. His father is a head accountant, a man who can be trusted, as he says, not without bitterness."

"I can understand that."

"They wanted to turn him into a lawyer or a doctor. He didn't have what it takes to go on with his studies. Nor did he want to go into the same firm as his father. Nothing original in that, as I told him.

"He works in an office. He lives alone. He has a reason for not getting married."

"Did he tell you what it was?"

"No, but I think I can guess."

Maigret, however, avoided saying anything more on that subject.

"I can't do anything but wait. He will undoubtedly call me up again tomorrow. I have to send his photograph to the papers on Wednesday afternoon."

"Why?"

"An ultimatum from the magistrate. He doesn't want to bear the responsibility of waiting any longer, he says."

"Are you hoping that . . ."

The telephone rang.

"It's your anonymous caller, Superintendent."

"Hello. Is that Monsieur Maigret? I'm sorry I hung up on you this morning. There are times when I think that nothing has any meaning any more. I'm like a fly beating against a windowpane trying to escape from the four walls of a room."

"You aren't in your office?"

"I went there. I was full of good intentions. They gave me an important file to take care of. When I opened it and read the first lines I asked myself what I was doing there.

"I was seized by a kind of panic and, under the pretext of going to the washroom, I went down the corridor. I barely took the time to grab my raincoat and hat from the hook as I went by. I was afraid someone would catch me, I felt as if I was being pursued."

At the beginning of the call Maigret had signaled to Janvier to pick up the second receiver.

"Where are you?"

"On the Grands Boulevards. I've been walking in the crowd for an hour. There are moments when I hate you, when I suspect you of doing it on purpose to drive me out of my mind, to get me little by little into a mental state in which there will be nothing I can do but give myself up."

"Have you been drinking?"

"How did you know?"

He spoke more forcefully.

"I had two or three brandies."

"You don't usually drink?"

"Only a glass of wine with meals, rarely a drink by itself."

"Do you smoke?"

"No."

"What are you going to do now?"

"I don't know. Nothing. Walk. I might sit in a café and read the afternoon papers."

"Have you sent any more letters?"

"No. I may write one more, but there isn't much more left for me to say."

"Do you live in a furnished room?"

"I have my own furniture, and I have the use of a kitchenette and bathroom."

"Do you do your own cooking?"

146

"I did cook my evening meals."

"And you haven't done so for several days?"

"That's right. I go home as late as possible. Why are you asking such pointless questions?"

"Because they help me to understand you."

"Do you do the same with all those who come to you?"

"That depends on the case."

"Are they so different from one another?"

"Men are all different. Why don't you come and see me?"

There was a nervous little laugh.

"Would you let me leave again?"

"I couldn't promise you that."

"Well, you see . . . I'll come and see you, as you say, when I have made a final decision."

Maigret almost told him of the magistrate's ultimatum, then he weighed the pros and cons and decided to remain silent.

"Good-bye, Superintendent."

"Good-bye. Don't let it get you down."

Maigret and Janvier looked at each other.

"Poor man," murmured Janvier.

"He's still fighting himself. He is quite lucid. He isn't cherishing any illusions. I wonder if he'll come before Wednesday."

"Didn't you get the impression that he had begun to waver?"

"He has been wavering since Saturday. Just now he is outside, in the sunlight, in the crowd where no one takes any notice of him. He can go into a café and order a brandy and they'll serve him without paying any attention to him. He can go and have dinner in a restaurant, or sit in the darkness in a movie house."

"I know what you mean."

"I'm putting myself in his place. From one hour to the next . . ."

"If he were to commit suicide, as you fear, it would be even more final."

"I know. But he must know that. I only hope he doesn't keep on drinking."

Light currents of chilly air drifted through the room and Maigret looked at the open window.

"Well, what about a drink?"

And a few minutes later they were both seated at the bar in the Brasserie Dauphine.

"A brandy," ordered the superintendent, which made Janvier smile.

Chapter **7**   Tuesday was a terrible day.
Nevertheless Maigret arrived at his office in high spirits.
It was such a truly spring day that he had walked all the
way from the Boulevard Richard-Lenoir, sniffing the air,
the smells from the shops, looking around from time to
time at the bright and gay dresses worn by the women.

"Nothing for me?"

It was nine o'clock.

"Nothing."

In a few minutes, in half an hour, one of the editors or
chief reporters would call him up to tell him about another letter written in block letters.

He expected it to be a decisive day. He was ready for it
and he laid his pipes out on his desk, chose one with care,
and went over to the window to light it, looking out at
the Seine, which sparkled in the morning sun.

When he had to go to the briefing, he had Janvier sit in
his office.

"If he telephones, get him to wait and come and get me
at once."

"Right, Chief."

There was no telephone call while he was in the director's office. There wasn't one by ten o'clock. There was
still none by eleven o'clock.

Maigret went through his mail, filled out forms, his
mind abstracted, and occasionally, as if to make the time
pass more quickly, he went in to the inspectors' office, tak-

ing care to leave the door open. Everyone knew he was worried and nervous.

The telephone which did not ring created a sort of vacuum that made him uneasy. He felt something lacking.

"Are you sure there has been no call for me, Mademoiselle?"

In the end it was he who called up the newspaper offices.

"Haven't you had any letter this morning?"

"Not this morning, no."

The day before, the first call from the Rue Popincourt man had come at ten minutes past noon. At noon Maigret did not go downstairs with the others. He waited until twelve thirty and once more asked Janvier, who was best informed on the case, to relieve him.

His wife did not ask him any questions. The answers were only too obvious.

Had he lost the game? Had he been wrong to trust to instinct? Tomorrow at that time he would have to go to see the magistrate and admit his defeat. The photograph would be printed in the papers.

What the devil could that idiot be doing? Maigret felt surges of anger.

"He was only trying to make himself interesting and now he has dropped me. Maybe he's laughing at my naïveté."

He went back to the Quai earlier than usual.

"Nothing?" he asked Janvier mechanically.

Janvier would have given a lot to have some good news to give him, for it upset him to see his chief in such a state.

"Not yet."

The afternoon was even longer than the morning. Maigret tried in vain to get up some interest in his routine work, using the time to deal with paperwork that was overdue. His heart wasn't in it.

He thought of all the possibilities and rejected them one by one. He even rang the police emergency first-aid section.

"You haven't been called to any suicides, have you?"

"Just a minute. There was one during the night, an old woman who asphyxiated herself, out by the Porte d'Orléans. A man threw himself into the Seine at eight o'clock this morning. We were able to save him."

"What age was he?"

"Forty-two. A neurotic."

Why was he doing all these things? He had done what he could. It was time to face reality. He wasn't hurt at having been fooled but at seeing that his intuition had been wrong. That meant that he was no longer able to make contact, and in that case . . .

"Damn, damn, and damn!"

He had said that at the top of his voice, alone in his office, and he picked up his hat and went, coatless and alone, over to the Brasserie Dauphine, where he drank two pints of beer one after the other, standing at the counter.

"No telephone calls?" he asked on his return.

By seven o'clock he had had no call and he resigned himself to going home. He felt heavy and was not at peace with himself. He took a taxi. He found no joy in the sunshine, nor in the colorful street noises. He could not even have said what the weather was like.

He started to climb the stairs heavily and stopped twice because he found himself a little out of breath. A few steps away from his landing, he saw his wife watching him come up.

She had been waiting for him as if she were waiting for a child coming home from school, and he was almost angry with her. When he got up to her, she merely said in a low voice:

"He's here."

"Are you sure it's he?"

"He told me so himself."

"Has he been here long?"

"Almost an hour."

"Weren't you afraid?"

Maigret suddenly had a retrospective fear for his wife's safety.

"I knew I wasn't in any danger."

They were whispering outside the door, which was shut.

"We talked."

"What about?"

"Everything . . . Spring . . . Paris . . . the little truck drivers' restaurants which are disappearing now . . ."

Maigret went in at last and saw, in the living room which was both dining room and sitting room, a man, still young, who stood up. Madame Maigret had taken his raincoat and he had put his hat on a chair. He was wearing a navy-blue suit and looked younger than he really was.

He forced himself to smile.

"Forgive me for coming here," he said. "I was afraid that over there, at your office, they wouldn't let me see you right away. One hears so many things . . ."

He must have been afraid of being beaten up. He was embarrassed. He searched for words with which to break the silence. He did not realize that the superintendent was as embarrassed as he.

"You're just as I imagined you would be."

"Sit down."

"Your wife has been very patient with me."

And, as if he had forgotten about it until that moment, he pulled a Swedish knife from his pocket and held it out to Maigret.

"You can have the blood analyzed. I haven't cleaned it."

Maigret put it down nonchalantly on a table and sat in an armchair, facing his visitor.

"I don't know how to begin. It's very difficult to . . ."

"I'll start by asking you a few questions. What is your name?"

"Robert Bureau. Bureau like a bureau, a desk. You might say it's symbolic, since my father and I . . ."

"Where do you live?"

"I have a little room on the Rue de l'Ecole-de-Médecine, in a very old house at the end of the courtyard. I work on the Rue Laffitte, with an insurance company. Or rather, I used to work there. That's all over with now, isn't it?"

He spoke those words with a melancholy resignation. He had calmed down and was looking at the restful surroundings as if he wished he might become part of them.

"Where do you come from?"

"From Saint-Amand-Montrond, on the Cher. There's a big printing firm there, Mamin and Delvoye, who do work for several publishers in Paris. That's where my father works, and to him the name Mamin and Delvoye is sacred. We lived in a small house near the Berry canal— my parents live there still."

Maigret didn't want to hurry him, to get to the important questions too quickly.

"You didn't like your town, then?"

"No."

"Why?"

"I felt stifled there. Everyone knows everyone else. When you walk down the street you can see the curtains at the windows twitching. I've always heard my parents saying:

" 'What would people say?' "

"Were you good at school?"

"Until I was fourteen and a half I was at the top of the class. My parents were so used to it that they scolded me if I had one mark less than perfect on my school papers."

"When did you start to be afraid?"

Maigret had the impression that the man he was talking to turned paler, that two little hollows appeared near his nostrils, and that his lips grew dry.

"I don't know how I've been able to keep the secret until now."

"What happened when you were fourteen and a half?"

"Do you know that region?"

"I've been through it."

"The Cher runs parallel to the canal. In places it's ten yards or so away from it. It's broad and shallow, with stones and rocks so that one can wade through it.

"The banks are covered with rushes, with willows, with bushes of all kinds. Especially around Drevant, a village about two miles from Saint-Amand.

"That's where the local children usually go to play. I didn't play with them."

"Why not?"

"My mother called them little hoodlums. Some of them used to swim in the river stark naked. Almost all of them were the children of workers at the press, and my parents made a great distinction between wage earners and white-collar employees.

"There were about fifteen of them, maybe twenty, who

played together. There were two girls among them. One of them, Renée, who must have been thirteen, was very well developed for her age and I was in love with her.

"I've thought a lot about all this, Superintendent, and I wonder if it would have happened anyway in different circumstances. I suppose it would. I'm not trying to find excuses.

"One boy, the pork butcher's son, made love to her in the bushes. I caught them unawares. They went to swim with the others. The boy was called Raymond Pomel and he had red hair like his father, whose shop my mother patronized.

"At one moment, he moved away from the others to relieve himself. He came close to me without knowing it and I took my knife out of my pocket. I released the catch and the blade flicked out.

"I swear I didn't know what I was doing. I struck several times and felt as if I was freeing myself from something. For me, at that particular moment, it was absolutely necessary—I wasn't committing a crime, or killing a boy. I was just stabbing. I went on stabbing him after he had fallen to the ground, then I went away quite peacefully."

He was animated and his eyes shone.

"They only discovered him two hours later. They hadn't noticed he wasn't with the group of twenty children any more. I had gone home after washing the blade in the canal."

"How was it that you had this knife when you were so young?"

"I had stolen it from one of my uncles some months earlier. I had a passion for knives. As soon as I had any money I bought one which I always carried in my pocket.

I saw this Swedish knife at my uncle's house one Sunday and I took it. My uncle looked for it everywhere without even thinking of me."

"Why did no one, your mother, for example, ever find it?"

"The wall of our house, on the garden side, was covered with Virginia creeper. Its thick growth framed my window. When my knife wasn't in my pocket, I hid it where the vine was thickest."

"Didn't anyone suspect you?"

"That's what surprised me. They arrested a bargeman, whom they had to release. They thought of all possible subjects, except a child. . . ."

"What was your state of mind?"

"To tell you the truth, I felt no remorse. I listened to what the women said gossiping in the street, I read the Montlucon paper, which spoke of the crime, without feeling myself in any way concerned.

"I watched the funeral procession go past without any emotion. For me, at that time, it already belonged to the past. To the inevitable. It had nothing to do with me. I wonder whether you can understand that? I think it's impossible to do so if one hasn't been through it oneself.

"I kept on going to school, where I had become abstracted and where my marks got lower and lower. I must have grown somewhat paler and my mother took me to our family doctor, who examined me perfunctorily.

" 'It's just his age, Madame Bureau. The boy is a bit anemic.'

"I think that I didn't feel as if I belonged to the real world. I wanted to run away. Not to run away from any possible punishment, but to get away from my parents, from the town, to go far away, anywhere. . . ."

"Aren't you thirsty?" asked Maigret, who was very thirsty himself.

He poured two brandies and water and held one out to his visitor, who drank avidly, draining his glass in one gulp.

"When did you realize what had happened to you?"

"You do believe me, don't you?"

"I believe you."

"I have always thought that no one would believe me. It happened without my noticing it. As time went on, I felt myself more and more different from other people. Stroking the knife in my pocket with my fingers, I would say to myself:

"'I've killed someone. No one knows about it.'

"I almost wanted to tell them, to tell my fellow pupils, my teachers, my parents, as one boasts of something one has done. Then, one day, I found myself following a girl along the canal. It was the daughter of one of the bargemen and she was going back to the barge. It was winter and it was already dark.

"I told myself that all I had to do was to run a few steps, to take my knife out of my pocket . . .

"Suddenly I began to tremble. I turned around without thinking and ran back to the houses at the edge of the town, as if I would feel safer there. . . ."

"Did that happen to you often after that?"

"When I was a child?"

"At any time at all."

"About twenty times. Most of the time I didn't have a particular victim in mind. I would be outdoors and suddenly I would think:

"'I shall kill him.'

"I remembered much later that when I was a child,

when my father hit me and sent me to my room to punish me, I used to growl the same thing:

" 'I'll kill him.'

"I wasn't necessarily thinking of my father. The enemy was all mankind, man in general.

" 'I shall kill him.'

"Would you mind giving me another drink?"

Maigret poured him one and poured one for himself at the same time.

"How old were you when you left Saint-Amand?"

"Seventeen. I knew I'd never pass my exams. My father couldn't understand and worried about me. He wanted me to go into the printing firm. One night I went off without saying anything, taking with me a suitcase and what little I'd saved. . . ."

"And your knife!"

"Yes. I've meant to get rid of it a hundred times and could never bring myself to do it. I don't know why. You see . . ."

He was looking for words to express himself. One could tell that he wanted to be as truthful and precise as possible, which was difficult for him.

"In Paris at first I was hungry and, like so many other people, I unloaded vegetables at Les Halles. I read the advertisements in the papers and I went everywhere that had an opening. That's how I got into an insurance company."

"Have you had any girl friends?"

"No. I got along, from time to time, with picking up a girl on the street. One of them tried to slip an extra bank note out of my wallet and I almost took out my knife. My forehead was drenched with sweat. I staggered out. . . .

"I realized that I had no right to get married."

"Were you ever tempted to?"

"Have you ever lived alone in Paris, without relatives, without friends, and have you gone back to your room in the evening, alone?"

"Yes."

"Well then, you'll understand. I didn't want to have friends, either, because I couldn't be frank with them without risking being imprisoned for the rest of my life.

"I went to the Sainte-Geneviève library. I devoured psychiatric treatises, always hoping to find an explanation. Of course I didn't have the background. When I thought that my case corresponded to a particular mental illness, I would then realize that I didn't have such and such a symptom.

"I became more and more distressed.

"*'I shall kill him . . .'*

"I ended up with these words on my lips and so I would run home and shut myself in and throw myself down on my bed. I would just lie there groaning.

"One evening a neighbor, a middle-aged man, knocked at my door. I took my knife out of my pocket mechanically.

"'What do you want?' I called through the door.

"'Are you all right? You're not ill? I thought I heard you groaning. I'm sorry.'

"He went away again."

Chapter 8   Madame Maigret appeared in the doorway and made a sign that Maigret did not understand, so far away was he from those surroundings, then she murmured:

"Would you come in here a minute?"

Back in the kitchen, she whispered:

"Dinner's ready. It's after eight. What shall we do?"

"What do you mean?"

"We have to eat."

"We haven't finished."

"Perhaps he could join us?"

He looked at her, amazed. For a second this proposal seemed quite natural to him.

"No. There mustn't be a properly set table, no family dinner. That would make him feel terribly ill at ease. Have you any cold cuts, any cheese?"

"Yes."

"Well, then, make some sandwiches and bring them in to us with a bottle of white wine."

"What is he like?"

"Calmer and more lucid than I had thought he would be. I'm beginning to understand why he didn't get in touch with me in any way all day. He needed to step back, to see things in perspective."

"See what things?"

"Himself. Did you hear any of what he said?"

"No."

"When he was fourteen and a half he killed a boy."

When Maigret went back into the living room Robert Bureau, embarrassed, muttered:

"I'm keeping you from your dinner, am I not?"

"If we were at the Quai des Orfevres I would send out for sandwiches and beer. There's no reason why I shouldn't do the same here. My wife is making sandwiches for us and she'll bring them in with a bottle of white wine."

"If only I had known . . ."

"If you had known what?"

"That someone could understand me. You must be an exception. The judge won't have the same attitude, or the jury. I've spent my whole life being afraid, afraid of stabbing someone else without meaning to.

"I have watched myself, so to speak, at all times, wondering if I wasn't about to have an attack—at the slightest headache, for example.

"I've consulted I don't know how many doctors. I didn't tell them the truth, of course, but I complained of violent headaches that were accompanied by a cold sweat. Most of them didn't take it seriously and prescribed aspirin.

"A neurologist on the Boulevard Saint-Germain did an electroencephalogram. According to him, I have no brain damage."

"Was that recently?"

"Two years ago. I almost wanted to tell him that I wasn't normal, that I was a sick person. Since he didn't find out for himself . . .

"When I went past a police station I wanted to go in and say:

"'I killed a boy when I was fourteen and a half. I'm afraid I may kill again. It ought to be cured. Shut me up and have someone take care of me.'"

"Why did you never do that?"

"Because I've read so many things. At almost every trial the psychiatrists give evidence and often they're laughed at. When they talk about diminished responsibility or mental deficiency the jury doesn't pay any attention. At best they get the sentence down to fifteen or twenty years.

"I forced myself to manage alone, to recognize when an attack was coming on, to run and shut myself up in my room. It worked, for a long time. . . ."

Madame Maigret brought them in a tray of sandwiches, a bottle of Pouilly-Fuissé, and two glasses.

"I hope that will do."

She went out quietly to eat alone in the kitchen.

"Help yourself."

The wine was cold and dry.

"I don't know if I'm hungry. There are some days when I eat hardly anything and others, on the contrary, when I'm ravenous. That may be a sign, too. I look for signs everywhere. I analyze all my reactions. I attach importance to my slightest thought.

"Try to put yourself in my place. At any moment I might . . ."

He bit into his sandwich and was the first to be surprised to see himself eating naturally.

"And I was afraid I might have been wrong about you. I had read in the papers that you were human and that you sometimes went against the Public Prosecutor's Office. On the other hand, I've heard of your interrogations keyed to make one sing—you treat the prisoner gently and kindly to make him feel at ease and he doesn't realize that you're dragging it all out of him."

Maigret couldn't help smiling.

"Not all cases are the same."

162

"When I telephoned you I weighed every one of your words, every one of your silences."

"You came in the end."

"I no longer had any choice. I felt my whole world falling apart. Wait! I'll make you a confession—yesterday, at one particular moment on the Grands Boulevards, I had the idea of attacking somebody, anybody, in the middle of a crowd, of striking out all around me, savagely, in the hope that someone would kill me.

"May I pour myself another glass of wine?"

He added, with rather sad resignation:

"I shan't drink any more wine like that for the rest of my life."

For a moment Maigret tried to imagine what Magistrate Poiret's expression would have been if he had been able to hear this conversation.

Bureau continued:

"There were three days of torrential rain. They often talk about the moon and its effect on people like me. I watched myself. I didn't notice that my impulses were stronger or more frequent at the time of the full moon.

"It is rather a certain intensity of the weather that has an effect. In July, for example, when it's very hot. In the winter when the snow is falling in huge flakes.

"You might say that nature has a period of crisis and . . .

"Can you understand?

"That rain that went on incessantly, the squalls, the sound of the wind rattling the shutters of my room, all that combined to put my nerves on edge.

"In the evening I went out and began to walk in the storm. After a few minutes I was soaked and I raised my head on purpose to get the lashing of the rain full in the face.

"I didn't hear the warning signal, or if I did I didn't obey it. I should have gone home instead of keeping on. I didn't notice where I was going. I walked and walked. At one particular moment my hand gripped the knife in my pocket.

"I saw the lights of a little bar in a dark little street. I heard footsteps in the distance, but that didn't worry me.

"A young man in a light-colored jacket came out, his long hair plastered to his neck, and the trigger was released.

"I didn't know him. I had never seen him before. I hadn't seen his face. I struck at him several times. Then, as I was going away, I realized that I hadn't yet reached the moment of release, and I went back to strike him again and to lift up his head. . . .

"That's why they talked about a madman. They also said a psycho case."

He stopped talking and looked around him as if he were surprised to find himself where he was.

"I really am mad, am I not? It isn't possible that I'm not ill. If only I could be given treatment. . . . That's what I've been hoping for for so long. But you'll see, they'll just send me to prison for life."

Maigret didn't dare answer.

"Aren't you going to say anything?"

"I hope they'll give you treatment."

"But you wouldn't count too much on it, would you?"

Maigret emptied his glass.

"Drink up. We'd better go straight over to the Quai des Orfèvres."

"Thank you for listening to me."

He emptied his glass in one swallow and Maigret poured him another.

———

Bureau wasn't very wrong. At the trial, two psychiatrists gave evidence that the accused was not insane in the legal sense of the word but that his responsibility was greatly diminished since he found it difficult to resist his impulses.

The defense counsel begged the jury to send his client to a mental hospital where he could be treated.

The jury accepted the attenuating circumstances, but still condemned Robert Bureau to fifteen years' imprisonment.

After which the judge, after coughing, pronounced:

"We realize that this verdict does not completely agree with the facts. At present, alas, we have no establishments where a man like Bureau may be given effective treatment while remaining under strict surveillance."

Standing in the box, Bureau looked for Maigret and gave him a smile of resignation. He seemed to be saying:

"That's what I foresaw, isn't it?"

When Maigret left the court his shoulders were a little more bowed.

Epalinges
April 21, 1969

Books by Georges Simenon
available in paperback editions
from Harcourt Brace Jovanovich, Inc.

The Accomplices
The Blue Room
The Cat
The Clockmaker
Maigret and the Killer
Maigret and the Madwoman
Maigret and the Man on the Bench
Maigret Sets a Trap
November
Sunday